BLACK OUT

BALLARAT CHARTER
LILA ROSE

Second Edition 2019

ISBN: 978-0648481690

To my readers, thank you for your support.
YOU ROCK!

CHAPTER ONE

CLARINDA

*T*hree weeks of hearing his voice and I was addicted. While my sister was busy doing whatever she had to do every Saturday for the past three weeks for her realty work, she dropped me off at a café so I wouldn't get in her way and annoy her. So for those three Saturdays, I had my ears glued to the door of that café, waiting for him to walk in and order his tall cappuccino. His voice was deep, rough and warming. His scent filled the room and made me want to wear leather and drink whatever men's cologne he wore so that I could have it surrounding me all the time.

Sex.

That word never really crossed my mind, mainly

because my first and *only* time was not worth remembering. I had been eighteen when I met *the unnameable,* and he had swooned his way into my life. I thought he was the one. He showered me with gifts and sweet words. Until I gave him my virginity. Then as soon as he'd donned the condom, stuck it in me—and Jesus, it had hurt so much, I was ready to punch the uncaring idiot in the throat— he'd thrust three times and grunted in my ear. The next day when I rang him, he said he didn't want to hang, that I was a lousy lay.

So anyone could understand why sex, lust or making love never crossed my mind.

Until him, the stranger in the café.

It sounded strange; I knew it did. I wasn't usually a stalker type of person, but it was a small enjoyment in my troubled life, and it wasn't harming anyone in return.

So yet another Saturday, and I found myself sitting in that café drinking a coffee and nibbling on a blueberry muffin, while I waited to get my pleasure for the day of hearing his voice.

The bell over the café door rang, heavy footsteps coming in and walking toward the front counter. I knew this with relative ease because every time I walked in, I'd counted the number of steps it took me to get to the counter to make my order. I'd also counted them to my usual table, the table my sister had shown me to on the very first time I had come here. She knew my counting game, so at least she knew from then on, I could make it in and to my seat without embarrassing myself.

I was sitting off to the left of the front counter, taking in a deep breath, and his manly scent soon filled my senses once again. I had to take my fill before he walked out like he always did.

What was funny was I'd never felt the need to do it with any other customer. I hadn't cared to. Still, when he walked in that first time, there was something about the way he walked, the way he talked and the way the room had quieted and people took notice of him.

It left me wanting to know him.

However, that was something I'd never have a chance of obtaining, especially when no one took notice of me these days.

My appearance was less than to be desired. My clothes were baggy and big, while my red hair was a mess, and I wore no makeup, and sunglasses sat on my nose.

His order was called. I heard him say a rumble of a 'Thank you' and then I waited for his retreating footsteps, back to the front door.

Only, for the first time, he didn't.

He wasn't walking out of the café; he was staying. I could tell when I heard his pounding footsteps coming my way. I smiled a little because I knew I'd appreciate taking in his alluring masculine scent a little longer.

"Hey, sugar, mind if I sit here?" he asked.

My lips pulled between my teeth. Was he talking to me? Was the place that full we'd have to share a table?

I tipped my head in his direction and said quietly, in case he wasn't talking to me, and I was about to make a fool out of myself, "I don't mind."

It's days like this I wish I could see. But I couldn't. My eyesight had been perfect until five years before, four days after my nineteenth birthday. After one tragic night —the night my older sister and I lost our parents.

On that horrid night, I ended up in a coma for a month, and when I woke, I could no longer see properly. My sister explained to me, once released from the hospital, that my visual impairment was caused by carbon monoxide poisoning from being in the fire. That and the loss was a result of emotional trauma from witnessing my parents burn to death. They'd been stuck behind a locked door and couldn't escape.

The pain from the loss of my parents hurt more than any side effect or injury. Five years, and I was still feeling that loss deep inside.

It was lucky my sister hadn't been there that dreadful night, or she also would be waking every night from the same nightmares still haunting me.

The chair opposite me grated across the floor as he pulled it out and set something on the table in front of him.

Sounds were my best friend these days.

"Three weeks," he stated.

"I'm sorry?" I uttered.

"Three weeks, baby. Three weeks I've been coming here every Saturday, waiting for you to come to me to make a move. But you never have, so I thought I would."

My eyes widened behind my glasses, my mouth ajar. He had shocked me to silence as my heart went haywire behind my loose tee.

"I s'pose I should be the one to introduce myself, now that I'm finally fuckin' here in front of you."

Quickly closing my gaping mouth, I brought my bottom lip between my teeth and bit down once again. I couldn't answer; so instead, I nodded.

"Name's Blue Skies."

A small smile tugged at my lips as I held back the inappropriate giggle. What were his parents thinking at the time they named him? I cleared my throat and whispered like it was a secret, "I'm Clarinda."

"Clarinda… Clary. I like it." I could hear the smile in his voice, and for some reason, it had me blushing. "Seems it's our first date, so I guess we should tell each other about us."

My head went back a little, again, shocked at his statement. So shocked, in fact, I laughed. "Are you sure you have the right person?" I asked after I controlled my laughter.

"Yes."

Puzzled, I asked, "How?"

"Because I've had my eyes on you for three damn

Saturdays. Waiting to catch your eye, waiting for you to get the courage to talk to me, but you haven't. So now, we do this my way."

"Your way?" I asked in a whisper.

"Yeah, sugar," he said softly. "My way."

Licking my suddenly dry lips, I then said, "You sure are...."

"Cocky? Great with words? Smart? Handsome?"

Smiling, I shook my head. "I wouldn't know. I can't see," I told him and removed my sunglasses, blinking in his direction.

He sucked in a sharp breath. "Damn, your eyes are beautiful like that."

My eyes widened, *yet again*. This man in front of me sure knew how to make an impression. I wasn't sure if I liked it. All right, I did. I guess I was more confused over why the man was saying those words to me.

Three weeks. His words rippled through my mind again.

Three weeks I've been coming here every Saturday, waiting for you to come to me to make your move. How was it... *he* possible? Was I dreaming?

Light footsteps approached our table, and a woman cleared her throat. "Hey, handsome."

Blue interrupted her to say to me, "See? I told you." I giggled. "What can I do for you, sweetheart?"

I snorted. Oh, God, he was a charmer to every lady.

"I have to go, but I just wanted to give you this," the woman said.

This was embarrassing; I just knew she was passing him her number. Even a strange woman could see it was weird Blue was sitting with me.

Actually, that was reality and it just smacked me in the face.

I stood up and said, "I'm leaving, as well. Why don't you take my seat?"

"No," Blue growled. "Sugar, sit your arse down. We're talking. And woman, you need to go. I don't want your number... ever." I was surprised he sounded disgusted.

Quietly feeling my way back into my seat, I sat across from him. The woman huffed and puffed, and then I listened to her retreating footsteps.

I wondered if he got that a lot. If many women picked him up wherever he went. It also made me want to know what he looked like, especially if that sort of thing *did* happen a lot.

"Stupid woman interupuring us," Blue grumbled.

"I'm sure you could still chase her." A grin tugged at my lips.

"You, shut it," he said with a smile in his voice. "Now, tell me about Clary."

I shrugged. What was happening was the weirdest situation I'd ever been in. No man had ever approached me before. "There isn't much to say really."

"What do you like to do?" he asked.

"Read—I mean, listen to audiobooks." I smiled. "What do *you* like to do, Blue?"

"I'd fuckin' love to know—" His phone rang, cutting him off. "Christ," he swore and answered it with a gruff, "What? Shit. Yeah, all right, I'm comin'." I heard him shut his phone and slam it to the table. "I have to go."

"That's okay."

"No, it ain't."

Without thinking, I uttered, "You're right. It isn't."

He groaned. "Shit, now I don't wanna leave, but if I don't we won't get this car out at the garage, and the dick has fucked it up even more." His chair was shifted back, meaning he stood. A finger trailed down my cheek. "Will you be here next Saturday?"

"I think so."

"I'll see you then, sugar."

THE FOLLOWING SATURDAY, my sister dropped me off. When I walked to the counter, the guy behind it said, "I have a message for you. Blue's sorry he can't make it, but he hopes you'll try to come back Monday and he'll be here." I smiled wide and nodded my thanks. Since I was at the café, I still had to sit and wait for my sister, so I ordered an iced coffee and blueberry muffin.

Even though I knew he wasn't coming, my heart still thumped hard every time the front door opened. Once my sister turned up, I was relieved; my poor heart needed the break. She led me out to the car and told me to get in.

"How was your day?" I asked Amy.

"Fine. Look, I'm not in the mood to chit-chat, just… zip it, okay?"

Sighing quietly so she wouldn't get upset by it, I nodded. I sat back in my seat, thought of Blue and contemplated how I was going to make it there on Monday.

I waited until the next day before I spoke to my sister. Amy was sitting in the living room. I made my way from my room down the hall, with my hands on the walls to guide me. In the living room, I counted the five steps to the couch; only I didn't get there. Instead, I tripped and fell to the carpeted floor on my hands and knees.

"What are you doing?" Amy yelled.

"Sorry, I, um… tripped." I felt around on the floor to see what had been laying there to trip me, but my hands ran over nothing but the carpet.

"There's nothing there. Get up," Amy snapped. I did, and I reached out to the couch and climbed from my knees to sit on it. "Was there something you wanted? Usually, you stay in your room."

Nodding, I asked, "I was hoping you could take me to the café on Monday."

"Why?" she huffed.

"I… um, I have to meet someone there."

"I'll see, okay? I have a lot to do to keep us fed and a roof over our heads."

She'd said that to me many times. I'd questioned her about it on a few occasions because I was sure our parents would have helped provide for us after their deaths. Not that I would want it, but since I was disabled, we needed it even more. Our parents were well off, so every time Amy would hiss back, 'They never left enough for all *your* hospital bills,' I never could understand that.

I knew I was a burden to her, so I nodded and said, "Okay, Amy." Even though everything inside me told me to fight with her, to demand she take me because God knew I didn't ask for much. Still, I said no more, knowing one day, I would have to get out from under my sister and learn to live again.

MONDAY CAME AND WENT. Amy said she was too busy to take me, and when I suggested a taxi, she yelled at me for wanting to waste our money on something so unnecessary. I felt terrible that I couldn't inform Blue I wouldn't be there like he had me. We didn't have a home phone; the only phone we had was Amy's mobile, and she had taken that with her. If I had a friend, I would have called one, but they all soon disappeared after the accident.

I could only hope he would be there on Saturday and would understand my situation.

Wednesday night, Amy came home from work and told me to get on a warmer coat because she needed to go food shopping. She only liked me to go so I could push the trolley. She hated doing it and laughed if I crashed into anything.

At the supermarket, I trolled along slowly while Amy took off ahead. Thankfully, the place was lit bright enough for me to see her shadowed, blurred form in front of me.

"Rinda, stay there. I'm just going to grab some stuff. You're going too slowly. I'll be quicker on my own." There was no point saying anything; her footsteps were already departing the aisle.

I felt awkward just standing there, so I turned to the shelves and pretended to look at what was in front of me. I didn't know how long I had been standing there, but suddenly, there was heat at my back and a whisper in my ear, "Why are you searching the condoms, sugar?"

No, God no. Blue was right behind me, and apparently, I was looking at condoms.

"Um," was all I could say.

"Were you thinkin' of buying them for me?"

Oh, my God!

Again, my reply was, "Um,"

He chuckled deeply. "I'm only teasin', baby," he whispered against my neck, and I swear he drew in a deep breath. With his hands on my hips, he turned me. I looked up his blurred form towards his head and smiled shyly, knowing I was blushing. "Where were you Monday, Clary?" he asked, his hands still on my hips, making it hard for me to concentrate.

"Um, I-I'm sorry, Blue. I couldn't make it, and I had no way of telling you."

"Sugar, I'm gonna tell you straight up. I wanna see more of you. You willin' for that to happen?"

"Yes," I responded immediately. Hell, did that sound too keen?

"Best fuckin' word. What's your number? I gotta jet, but I need your number, baby."

I rattled off my sister's mobile and then added, "It was nice seeing you."

"You, too. Fuck, you, too. Take care, sugar, and we'll talk soon, yeah?"

"Yes." I smiled.

Later that night, I ended up telling my sister all about Blue. I think she noticed how excited I was when I talked about him, but I got nothing from her other than, "We'll see if he rings. Not many men would want such a burden in their life, Rinda. I hope you know that."

Deflated, I went back to my room, hoping Blue would prove my sister wrong.

CHAPTER TWO

ONE MONTH LATER

CLARINDA

I was sitting in the passenger seat of the car, waiting for my sister while she ran an errand. It was a month after I saw Blue at the supermarket. He hadn't called, so I guessed my sister had been right. He hadn't even shown the times I went to the café again. Why did he act as though he liked me enough to call? Had I said something that night in the supermarket to change it? No, I couldn't have; he was the one who asked me for my number. I shook my head, attempting to shake the thoughts away.

The sun was shining brightly in the car that late afternoon, so I wound down my window to let the breeze through. The sounds of the outside world grew louder with vehicles driving near our parking spot at the side of the road. People walked up and down the pathway beside the car. I only wished I could see it. Unfortunately, like always, my eyes only managed a shadowy outline of things.

I tilted my head toward the breeze more and saw an outline of a building. What that building was, I had no clue.

Soon, I found myself blinking away tears as I thought of my most recent doctor's appointment, which I had just the day before. Even though I had been seeing that doctor for nearly four years, I still felt uncomfortable around him. His touch left me feeling dirty for some reason. Though, my sister swore he was the best in town and was the perfect doctor to try and help us fix my eyes.

Three years later, and I was still waiting for the right answer.

His words from yesterday ran through my mind. *"You're coming along fine, Clarinda. Just give it time."*

Time was all I had.

Amy still refused to let me work, to let me do anything, really. If I tried, we ended up in an argument. I was born an independent yet shy woman, and I was sick of relying on my sister for help. I was twenty-four, for god's sake.

I shifted in my seat, so my head was closer to the window and wondered why my sister was taking so long. She said she'd only be a moment.

"What the fuck are you looking at?" I heard yelled in a harsh voice from somewhere close.

Ignoring it, I went back to blinking at nothing until a dark form loomed in front of me. I jumped, hitting my head on the car roof.

"I said, what the fuck are you looking at, bitch?" A shadow of a manly-shaped hand reached in and gripped my hair, pulling my head toward the window.

"Please, please," I begged. "I wasn't staring at anything."

"You wanna be up in my business, watching what went down? I'll give you a better taste of it, slut." He shook my head roughly with the hand still in my hair.

I reached up with both hands and grabbed his wrist, trying to pull free. "I didn't see anything. I *can't* see anything. Please, I'm blind. You've got it wrong."

"Bullshit. I don't give a fuck either way." He jerked my head again, and it banged into the top of the window frame. His stinking, hot breath blew against my face as he leaned closer. "You are a looker. I think a lesson needs to be learned."

"No!" I yelled. "Please." My body shook with fright.

My hands sweated and my heart leaped from the thought of what could happen. *Amy, please hurry, please!*

"Shut the fuck up," he hissed. Suddenly, my hair was

freed, and I flopped back ungracefully. My hands felt for the seat as I straightened myself.

What now? Dread filled my stomach. I didn't know what was going on, why all of a sudden he was silent, but then came the sound of my door being opened, causing me to jump. I threw my arms out in front of me, waving them around.

"No, please!" I cried.

A hand clamped around my thigh, his grip painful. "Come on, bitch. Take off your pants and spread 'em." He tugged on my sweatpants. My hands fought his hold.

"Stop, no. Stop. Amy!" I yelled.

He kept swatting my hands away and grumbling about something under his breath.

Then I heard another manly call, and then a thumping sound. The hands which were on me fell away.

"Leave her alone, Henry," the new person growled.

"Fuck off, Blue. This is none of your business."

Blue?

"I think it is. The lady doesn't want to be touched. If you don't back the hell off, I'll make you."

"Shit, she wasn't worth it anyway," the first man grumbled.

Silence, and then retreating footsteps. With shaking hands, I felt for the door to close it, but my hands came against a hard, warm wall. Bouncing back in my seat, I retracted them quickly.

"You all right, sugar?" my saviour asked.

Blue. Oh, God, it *was* Blue.

I nodded. Clenching my trembling hands, I whispered, "Yes." I was still tense, unsure if I was completely safe.

The thump of my door closing had me jumping once again. "He won't bother you again. You waitin' on someone?"

"My sister," I whispered.

Does he not remember me?

My heart plummeted. Maybe he didn't want to recognise me. That could be why he didn't call. I never left a good enough impression on him for him to care.

"Why didn't you call me?" I bravely asked through the silence.

"I did, Clarinda. I was told you didn't want anything to do with me."

My eyes widened. "No... I-I'd never say that, Blue."

"Fuck. Your sister...."

My heart pounded into my throat as the driver's side door opened beside me. I turned to it as my sister spat, "What have you done now, Clarinda?"

Tears pooled in my eyes. The adrenaline rush I had started to wear off. "Nothing, Amy. This...." I gestured with my hand in the general direction of the man I had thought of so frequently, "....is Blue. Um, I've talked about him. He, ah, just now helped me. Someone tried to attack me."

She snorted. "You probably brought it on yourself."

"She didn't," Blue clipped. My heart warmed.

"Whatever," Amy responded and started the car.

"You going to be okay?" he asked.

I nodded and looked toward the window. "I think so." I reached my hand out. He must have sensed I was having trouble finding him, so he placed his hand in mine. I squeezed it, my heart beat faster from the warmth and thrill of touching him. "Thank you," I whispered. "Can… would you meet me at the café? I'll be there next Saturday."

"I'll be there, sugar. Count on it." I could hear the smile in his voice. It had my cheeks heating and an urgent need to actually see him. I desperately wished to know what he looked like, what he felt like under my touch. I'd lay awake countless nights debating the colour of his eyes, not knowing if they were light or dark. While I'd heard his smile when he spoke, I was eager to see it and half-expected to find a dimple. Regardless of what he would look like to the outside world, none of it really mattered. His voice alone held me captive. As long as a man was kind to his woman like my father was to my mother, nothing else mattered.

"Hand in the car. We've got to go," Amy said.

I hadn't realised I was still gripping Blue's hand, but once I let go, I felt the warmth from his hold disappear. The reality of what happened slipped into my mind, and the smile fell from my face. Before I could say any more to Blue, Amy put the car into drive and took off.

I wanted her to turn the car around so I could find that warmth again, find the safety I felt around a man I hardly knew. I curled my arms around my waist, leaned my head back and closed my eyes thinking of the sweet yet hard, delicious tone of Blue's voice and found some comfort from it.

"What were you thinking, talking to a stranger?"

Sighing, I turned my head toward my sister. "He's not a stranger, Amy. He did help me." I shuddered at the thought of that dirty man touching me. "A man was attacking me."

"Well, what did you do for that to happen?"

"Nothing," I uttered.

"See, this is why you need me around all the time. You keep getting into trouble, and in the end, *I* keep having to save you."

Only that time, it wasn't her.

However, she was right. Over the past six months, I'd had many little accidents, and Amy had always been there for me. I had to admit—if Blue hadn't shown up, at least I knew my sister would have. She was always there.

Though, the accident which had just occurred was the worst I'd ever had... if I could call it an accident. The others before that were small incidents—a trip, a burn, stubbing my toe—and I'd been abused verbally many times on the street.

Still, it all gave me enough pause to think about how I would be lost without Amy. It actually made me sick to my stomach at the thought of fending for myself while in my condition. Yes, we annoyed each other, and yes, she could be downright mean, but she changed her ways to fit me into her life when I was nineteen and she was twenty-two. Without her, I wouldn't have had much of a life at all.

Okay, that wasn't entirely true.

People who were completely blind and saw nothing but blackness still coped. They used their other senses or had the help of guide dogs. There were many possibilities. I'd even suggested all those things to my sister at the start, told her I wanted to live on my own and learn to live with my disability. She wouldn't have it.

After what happened a few moments before, I wasn't sure I was ready to do any of that anymore.

I was scared something like that could happen again.

What would I do if I was on my own, walking down the street, and I didn't know someone was following me? I could turn a wrong corner and be trapped. I could witness something I never knew I was observing and be in a mess like I was earlier. So many things could happen. It was hard being with my sister all the time, but the thought of being without her scared me more.

At least I had my daily outings to the library while Amy worked. Those I really enjoyed, especially since I hardly sat on my own anymore. Not that it bothered me to sit on my own; at least I was able to listen to so many wonderful stories. Until, that was, Julian decided he had to know me. That had been about four months before. From that day forward, I would get several visits in the library from him.

He made me laugh, he made me smile, and the world seemed that much brighter with him around in it.

I also met his friend, Deanna, who works there. That had only been in the past two months, and still, we hadn't encouraged each other to talk openly. I was slowly warming up to her, but it was hard because of how snappy and annoyed she seemed to be all the time. The customers usually got a reprieve from her mouth, but if she came over to the table to grumble about something, look out. I had never in my twenty-four years heard a woman swear so much in my life. What was comical about it, though, was when Julian would bait her, she'd get frustrated and tell him where to go... explicitly. Julian didn't care. I loved to hear their interactions. Anyone could tell the 'family love' they had for each other.

At least I have someone *who's happy to see me.*

I turned my head toward Amy as she drove. Knowing my sister, her brows would be drawn, her jaw would be clenched, and her hands would be tight around the steering wheel. She was annoyed by me, for the attention I received but didn't want. I was her embarrassment.

Why had she told Blue I didn't want anything to do with him when he called? Was she jealous? Or maybe she just didn't want to see me hurt?

I wasn't sure, and I didn't want to ask. It would just end in a fight.

Everything was so confusing. One moment, I wanted to be independent and try to make Amy see I could do things for myself, and then the next, I found myself scared of what it would be like without her.

Confusion didn't accurately describe the chaos of my emotions.

I wanted to fight back and have my independence, and I wanted my sister to treat me with respect instead of a piece of poo under her shoe...then again, I was scared of so many things, which was why I clammed up so many times and said nothing, even though I regretted it every time.

However, what I *was* confident about was that Amy wasn't simply annoyed at me; rather, she truly hated me.

That hurt more than what the foul-breathed man tried to do to me.

My sister, my own family, hated me because I was useless. At least, that was how I felt.

CHAPTER THREE

ONE WEEK LATER

BLUE

A grumble came from my chest. I was at the compound where my brothers wanted to put together a BBQ for Wildcat. It'd been a month since she'd given birth to Drake and Ruby, so we wanted to celebrate it with them. I was happy to be there, but I couldn't help feeling like shit. I'd just met Killer's—my brother in arms —new woman, and wished it had been me to lose that bet. Then, at least I would have met Ivy, and it'd be me with a new, *serious* woman on my arm, instead of the sluts who just wanted biker cock.

I'd been over that scene for some time, ever since Zara came into our lives. The way she was, her craziness and uniqueness had me wanting her in ways I'd never felt before… but she only had eyes for Talon, and the feeling was mutual. I was happy for them, but fuck, I wanted that happiness for me, too.

A vision of Clarinda filled my head, but I quickly shook it off. She hadn't shown that morning at the café, or since then. Like a sucker, I'd been back a couple of times, just in case. I didn't know what her game was, but it sure as fuck wasn't going to be playing me.

Still, her beauty took my breath away.

Shit, I sounded like a fucking pansy. Next, I'd be consulting Julian on what to wear and whatnot.

I needed to get my head together, snap the fuck outta my funk and get the thought of finding a woman out of my brain. There weren't many good women out there; they were rare and I guessed my luck in finding one had run the fuck out.

Clary. Oh, hell the fuck no. I was not going to start pining over some blind bird I'd met a few times. No matter how hard she made my cock from just her voice, her laugh and her looks.

It was just luck I was happenin' along that day and witnessed Henry, a local druggie, abusin' her.

I saw fuckin' red and strode over, ready to break the dick's neck. It was bloody fortunate for him he quickly backed down.

It was obvious Clary was going through her own Hell, and it was probably a Hell I shouldn't be involved in. I'd wondered a few times why she hid her banging body behind plain clothes and left her hair scruffy. What concerned me was it also looked like she hadn't slept in days.

Still, she was gorgeous.

No, I had to get her outta my head. She was the one who stood *me* up. Besides, there wasn't any way I'd be seeing her again. I wasn't one who chased.

Even if I want to.

Christ, no, I needed someone stable.

Jesus, have a listen to yourself. Fuckin' pansy. Maybe I should just get my arse-crack waxed and be done with it.

Scrubbing my hand over my face, I walked out the back to cooking, laughing and chatting. I made my way over to Talon, Griz, Killer, Stoke, and Memphis, who were chillin' while cooking on the grill.

"You over your little spat, princess?" Stoke grinned. I'd walked off before, after meeting Ivy, saying I'd missed out again on a good woman 'cause I knew I had, which meant the fucker was teasing me about it.

"Screw you," I growled low, and my brothers laughed. We stood around while waiting for the meat to cook and talked about business, ridin' and just shit, really. My eyes kept looking over at the women and kids. They all seemed happy. A sick feeling started in the pit of my stomach as I witnessed the fuckin' loving looks between partners. Even the new couple, Killer and his missus.

Shaking my head, I looked to the ground. I needed to get out of there and laid.

"Hey, Blue."

I glanced up to see Hell Mouth approaching with a smile on her face. She was smiling a lot these days, and it was good to see. She was also less of a bitch. *That* was definitely good to see.

"What's up, Hell Mouth?" I asked, turning toward her as she stopped in front of me.

"I need a favour."

"Darlin'," Griz growled at his woman.

Obviously, she was up to something. Chuckling to myself, I asked, "Oh, yeah, what?"

"You see, my car's gonna be getting fixed the next few days. I need someone to come to the library to pick me up."

My eyes widened and then lowered into a glare. I looked to Griz and saw him trying to hide his grin. "Hell Mouth, you've got a man for that sorta shit. I ain't a taxi service."

She rolled her eyes at me and sighed. "My *man* is busy."

"And I'm not?" I questioned.

"Blue, don't be an arse. Just come get me Tuesday from the library."

I rubbed the back of my neck as I wondered why

there was a sudden urgency to get me to the goddamn library. I looked up at her and smiled. "Can't anyway. I'm heading outta town for a couple of days."

Griz, Talon and the rest of my brothers cracked up laughing as Deanna placed her hands on her hips and glared at all of us. Her plan—whatever it had been—had failed.

"Fine, whatever," she snapped and walked off.

I turned to Griz and asked, "What was that about?"

Chuckling, he replied, "Don't worry about it, brother. No doubt she'll keep trying, no matter what."

"Maybe you should just get it the fuck over with and go to the library," Talon suggested.

"Nah, I'll leave her stewing for a while. It'd be good for Griz."

Griz snorted. "Yeah, thanks, dick."

The laughter started all around, and once it stopped, Killer asked, "You actually goin' out of town?"

"Yeah, it's about time I visited my ma and brother."

All faces turned serious. Talon sent me a chin lift.

My mum lived an hour away. Lived—I couldn't really call it that, more *survived*. She was mentally unstable and became that way seventeen years ago when my father tried to suffocate her while she was pregnant with my brother. Due to the lack of oxygen, my brother was born a little slower than normal. I smiled at the thought of him. Jason was still a bright little shit, outsmarting me all the time.

It was damn lucky I was visiting the night it happened, or I wouldn't have walked in on the fucker and gotten the chance to beat the crap out of him before he was taken to jail. *After* I had taken care of Mum and she was whisked away in the ambo. He was a drunk, a gambler, and just a mean motherfucker. Always had been. Throughout my childhood, I witnessed many beatings he gave my mum, and then received them myself when I got around the age of six. I never understood why she stayed with him. I begged her to leave...but she didn't. Since then, she was just a shell of the lovin' person she used to be.

Jason, who was turning eighteen in six months, lived with Mum still, but they also had forty-year-old Adele, Mum's full-time caregiver, living with them. At least I knew if Jason started any shit, Adele would put him back in line. If not, she'd call me, and I'd fix it.

"When you headin' off?" Stoke asked.

I shrugged. "In the next couple of days."

"Mind if I join you?" We all looked to Memphis. He was the oldest out of the bunch at the age of fifty-two and had been a part of Hawks even before Talon took over. He was one of the ones who was glad as fuck Talon changed the club's ways. He was a good man, but one I never really spent much time around.

"Sure," I answered.

"Cool, Talon wants me to check the Hawks charter in Caroline Springs."

"No worries. We'll head there first before hittin'
Mum's place."

Memphis choked on his sip of beer. "You want me to
come to your ma's place?"

Scrunching my nose up, I said, "Uh, yeah."

"I can wait at the club for ya."

"Nah, brother. I'm staying a night or two. Ma's got a
heap of room. We'll crash there instead of the
compound."

He shrugged. "All right."

Stretching, I said, "I'm gonna head off. Got a need for
a ride." Maybe sittin' on my Harley while I rode through
the streets was just what I needed to clear my head.

"No worries, brother. Thanks for showin'," Talon said.

Sending a chin lift to them, I quickly said goodbye to
everyone else. Bloody Nancy hugged the shit outta me.
That woman was full the fuck on. I even had to dodge
Julian as he tried to lay one on me. I didn't know what
was up with the people, but I was glad I was getting outta
there for a few.

CHAPTER FOUR

TWO WEEKS LATER

CLARINDA

*H*e hadn't shown, yet I was the one still thinking of him. I was sure I never crossed his mind, so why couldn't I get him out of my head? Why didn't he show? Maybe something had happened, and just in case something had, I went back the following Saturday. Amy had dropped me off and waited in the car, reading while I waited for a man I could possibly care for, only he didn't show.

At least the past couple of weeks had been better for Amy and me. I did my best not to annoy her too much. I made sure I was out of her way all the time, and when she asked me to meet her out front of the library every day, instead of her coming in, I did. She said she hated the sight of the fag (her word, not mine) who was always with me.

So when Friday came, and I was so engrossed in the conversation Julian and I were having about our favourite actors, I hadn't realised the time. Plus, my watch's alarm didn't ring, announcing that my fun time had to end. That was why I didn't expect the slap to the back of my head. The force behind it made my head swish forward, and if Julian's hand hadn't made it to my forehead to stop its descent, my face would have hit the table.

"Hey," Julian hissed.

"Shut it, fag."

I sat straighter and turned to my sister's angry voice. "Amy, what's going on?"

She snapped with venom. "You stupid bitch, I'm always wasting my time on you." She slapped the back of my head again. It hurt so much my hands flew up to hold it. "Why weren't you out front? You're supposed to be out front, so I don't have to waste my damn time coming in to get your sorry arse."

I cringed and listened to Julian's chair scrape back on the floor. He was standing, no doubt to defend me. Just as I was about to tell him not to worry, I heard another slap, but that time it was behind me, skin-on-skin.

"Let go of my hand, bitch," Amy barked.

A woman's evil chuckle erupted; it was Deanna. "You hit her one more time, and I will rip your tits off and shove them down your throat," she growled.

"Get lost. It's none of your business."

"You just made it my business by hittin' Clarinda."

I hadn't been sure Deanna even remembered my name, yet she was defending me. *Why?*

"*Rinda*, let's go," Amy snarled my nickname. She pulled back my chair with a force I never knew she had. I almost tumbled out when a feminine hand caught my arm. Deanna again.

"I think *you* should go," Deanna said flatly. I knew she was talking to my sister, not me. "Clarinda is staying."

"No, it's okay," I said, trying to calm the situation as I stood from my chair.

"Clary, honey lumpkin', no one should lay a hand on you, even if she is blood," Julian said softly from my side. I hadn't even heard him walk around the table. As Deanna and Amy traded hostile words, Julian came in closer.

"Please, she doesn't mean it. She must have had a bad day," I uttered.

"Sweetheart, you can't leave with her when she's like that, not after what we just saw her do to you," he pleaded.

It pleased me he cared, yet saddened me they witnessed Amy striking out at me. Amy had only hit me a few times in the past when she was livid. It was how I learned to keep quiet when she was in a mood as she was.

"I'll be fine," I said and grabbed for his hand which was on my arm. I gave it a reassuring squeeze.

I felt him shift. He overturned my hand and placed something hard and rectangular-shaped in it. He whispered, "It's a phone and charger. I've meant to give it to you the last couple of times I've seen you. My little melon, I want you to have it, no argument. Any time you need anything, just press one; it'll call me straight away. It's old-school, none of this touchscreen crap. You can't go wrong. Test it later when you're alone; feel it out."

Tears filled my eyes; this sweet man really cared for me. I bit my bottom lip and held back my overwhelming urge to sob in his arms. Instead, I nodded and snuck the phone and charger, which was wrapped around it into my bra, where I knew it wouldn't fall out or be seen, and where I could always feel it against me. Thankfully, it was compact enough it wouldn't stand out.

"Fuck you, bitch. Clarinda, we're leaving, *now*," Amy hissed, grabbing my arm roughly and dragging me from the library.

The drive to our four-bedroom home was silent. I didn't like it one bit. As soon as Amy pulled in to our driveway, she quickly got out. I climbed out more slowly, waiting with a sick feeling in my stomach for the fight which was going to occur.

It came as soon as we entered our lounge room. Our

house, or should I say Amy's house—she reminded me enough that it was hers—always smelled of fresh flowers and honeydew. I had always felt comforted being in there, but as soon as the next words left her mouth, I felt nothing but bitterness and cold.

"You're to never go to the library again. I don't like those people, and it would be better for you to not be around them."

"Amy, please, they're my friends."

"No!" she screamed. "They're users. You will do as you're told—"

"Amy," I interrupted. "I'm twenty-four years old. I have every right to be where I want and with whom," I explained.

She laughed menacingly. "You don't. Well, not unless you want me to turn you out if you don't listen to me."

My back straightened at her threat. "If that's the way you want it, I'll go."

She sighed deeply, I heard her move, and then she was beside me, taking my hand in hers. "Rinda, you know I would never want you gone." I found her sugar-sweet tone suspicious. "I just worry about you all the time. We both need time to calm down. How about while I make dinner, you go have a bath or something?"

Her sudden change in attitude had my head spinning. For the first time, the thought that Amy knew something or was up to something ran through my mind.

Numbly nodding, I made my way down the familiar

hall, feeling with my hands against the walls to the bath-room across from my bedroom. Opening the door, I walked over to the bath and turned on the taps. While the tub filled, I went back to the door and locked it. Going to the sink to lean against it, I pulled the phone from my bra. I could see the outline of something in my hand, though even my hand was blurred. *This is going to be harder than I thought.*

Pressing a button at the top, I put it to my ear, only nothing happened. I tried again, and that time I jumped when it made a sound. I looked up to the door, listening intently. No footsteps approached; Amy hadn't heard. I sighed with relief.

Taking a breath, I closed my eyes and ran my fingers over all the buttons. From what I remembered when I was younger, these types of phones had a call and end button up at the top, and then in the middle was the system button. I felt and found them. The number one button should be just below the call button. My thumb ran over it, so I went back and pressed it.

"Are you okay, sugarplum?" Julian voice called out.

A relieved smile slipped onto my lips. "Yes," my voice hitched. I wished I was at the library, with Julian there beside me. So many thoughts and emotions ran crazed through me.

"Oh, sweet cherry pie, are you sure you're okay?"

Clearing my throat, I answered, "Sorry, I am. It's just good to hear your voice."

"Yours too, buttercup."

I giggled. "Buttercup, I like that one. My dad used to call me that all the time."

"Then that's what I'll call you from now on. I'm adopting you as my daughter."

Laughing quietly, I said, "Julian, you can't. I'm too old."

He scoffed. "Oh, bull, how old are you?"

"Twenty-four."

"See? I'm thirty-nine. I could be your daddy if I had a monster back at fifteen."

Smiling, I said, "You're crazy."

"Only the best are, buttercup. One day or night, Clary, I'd love to know how you came about living with your sister."

I bit my bottom lip. "One day," I uttered. Lifting my head, I turned it sideways toward the door, so I could hear over the running water. My sister was approaching. "I have to go."

"Talk soon," Julian replied, and then he quickly hung up.

I hid the phone in my top again and went over to turn the taps off just as my sister knocked on the bathroom door.

"Yes?" I called.

"How long are you going to be? Dinner will be ready in half an hour."

"I'll make sure I'm out by then."

She didn't reply. I listened to her steps fall away from the door and back down the hall. I touched the phone through my tee. Such a small item was going to be my lifeline. One day, I had to be brave and get out from under my sister.

"Mum, Dad, please, I can't find the key. You have to get out!" I screamed through the door as the heat from the fire licked my body. I bent over as another coughing fit overtook me.

"Buttercup, you have to go. Get out of the house!" Dad yelled from the other side of the door.

"No, Dad. No, break the door down," I cried. Though, I knew he couldn't. The door was reinforced to keep others out, to protect Dad's work and safe.

"Baby girl," Mum called, "you need to listen to your father for once and get out. Please, for us, Clarinda. For us."

"No, no, Mum, I can't. I just need to find the key." Coughing, I frantically searched on the side table next to Dad's office door, where a key had been hidden only days ago. However, it was now missing.

It was becoming hotter and hotter by the second. My eyes stung, and my chest hurt, not only from the smoke but from the thought of not helping my parents. I fought the tears and distress and kept grabbing at things. It was hard to see through the thickness of the stinking smoke.

"Clarinda Glass, you need to leave, now," Dad ordered, his voice thick with emotion. Mum coughed badly. I could hear it clearly through the thick door because I was so close.

"My baby," Mum said after she got her breath.

I sank to the floor, to my hands and knees, and kept saying over and over, "No."

"We love you, Clary, so much. Please, tell your sister that, too," Dad said.

Trying to suck in a breath was hard; everything was so hard. I pounded the floor with my fist, but it was a pitiful punch. I was fading, and there wasn't anything I could do for my parents. "I love you both... l-love you," I whispered as my body flopped sideways.

Out of nowhere, my body was lifted from the floor. I opened my heavy lids to see a man in a mask. "You're okay, darling."

I tried to tell the fireman, "M-my parents, they're—" but I was too late because that was when my world exploded.

My body bolted upright as I gasped for breath. *Oh, God.* I had that same dream nearly every night, and parts still puzzled me. Why couldn't my parents unlock the door from the inside? Had something been keeping them in there? And why couldn't I find the key? Someone had to have moved it, but who? We had many workers throughout the house. My dad was a lawyer, a very powerful one, and we lived our lives with a lot of money. Had an employee betrayed them for some reason? Killed them?

The answers were lost to me, though. The explosion which rocked the house that night took all of them away. There was no proof of anything, except what had caused the fire. Apparently, the gas fireplace in the room next to my father's office had been faulty and caused a misfire, leaking small amounts of gas into the room. What lit the gas was the candle my mum loved to burn on the mantelpiece. The drapes went up first, and then the pressure built until it went *boom*.

The only problem with that… my father had recently had that fireplace checked a week before it happened.

I begged the police, my sister, and the firefighters for them to look into it more. They did but came up with nothing.

Bang!

A noise came from outside of my room, causing me to jump and clutch my quilt tighter to me.

"Shit, I just dropped something. Hang on, I'll check if she's still sleeping."

Quickly laying back, I pulled my cover up to my nose and feigned sleep. Amy opened my door and must have looked in, because then I heard, "She's still sleeping." She paused, and that was when I knew she was on the phone. I was glad no one else was with her. She closed my bedroom door. "What? No, she needs to be scared into wanting to stay with me. I can't have her questioning about leaving. We need the money we get from being her caregiver."

My eyes widened, and I held my breath as I listened. Unconsciously, my hand sought out the phone under my pillow.

"I don't care if you have things to do. I want this done

tomorrow. Scare her, or you won't see me or the money again. Got it?" her voice drifted down the hall. I threw the covers back and ran to the door with my hands out in front of me so I wouldn't knock into it and make a sound. I leaned my ear against it and listened. "Good, I'll see you tomorrow."

Holy hell. What just happened? What had I just heard? My hand went to my chest, my heart beating rapidly. It was going so fast it hurt in my chest.

My sister… Amy. Was she asking someone to scare me? *Shit, shit, shit.* I leaned over, supporting my weight with my hands on my knees, and tried to calm myself enough to think clearly.

She wanted me here for the money. She didn't care. Damn, she didn't care. She was prepared to have someone scare me into staying.

Anger overrode my feelings, even though I wanted to collapse to the ground, to freak out and cry from the hurt.

She was my sister, for fuck's sake.

My sister!

Stumbling back to my bed, I reached under my pillow and pulled out the phone. I needed help, and Julian was the only one who could.

I lifted the phone to my ear as I pressed one.

CHAPTER FIVE

ONE WEEK EARLIER

BLUE

*T*he visit to my mums was postponed until Ivy, and the shit that had come her way had passed. Thank fuck we got the dickhead who had done it to her before he could do more damage. Still, he'd caused enough to warrant a beating from Killer and Stoke while us brothers stood by and watched. It sucked arse the dude was gonna be breathing easy on the inside of a prison cell. At least we had a few other brothers on the inside, as well; I'm sure Dr. Fuck-up was gonna have a dandy time trying to stay alive.

The hour ride to Caroline Springs wasn't enough. I had a need to keep going, keep the breeze blowing and the sweet rumble between my legs and the thoughts of a certain redhead out of *my* head. But Memphis was with me, and Talon still wanted him to check in with the Hawks charter first.

We pulled through the wire gates and up to the front of their compound. The place was trashed. Kegs, cans, and bottles were littered everywhere. Not only that, but the grounds were unkempt. It looked like shit. No wonder Talon wanted Memphis down there, besides the fact that Motley, the president, hadn't been returning Talon's calls. Talon was the main head-honcho to four charters around Australia, and he was getting sick of the crap he had to deal with when a new president was sworn in. Motley hadn't been in the prez's seat for that long, three months really, after the old prez got shot, beaten and killed by a rival club.

None of the fuckers believed we no longer dealt in guns, drugs, and women. They still fucking thought they had to fight us for the territory. Well, they did, and we fought back harder because we just wanted our area clean. Especially since more and more brothers were settling down.

Climbing off my Harley, I looked to Memphis. "Christ, what the fuck are we walking into?" he growled.

Shaking my head, I said, "I don't know, man, but it ain't gonna make us happy."

"Agreed. Let's get it over with then."

With our helmets laid on our Harleys, we walked across the paved drive to the front door. I swiftly pulled the door open, and the scent of hooch, pussy, sweat, and beer hit our noses. I fought the urge to dry-heave; the place fuckin' stunk.

"Shit, when was the last time they cleaned this joint?" Memphis complained as we stalked down the hall to the main party area. Once we were through, my eyes widened. The floor, bar, couches… dammed everywhere was littered with bikers and sluts.

"What the fuck did they do," I asked Memphis. "Have a super-orgy or somethin'?"

"Christ if I know," he growled.

Sure, us bikers liked to party, but we still prefered to keep a clean ship to do so. The things going on in that place were not how we run things. It wouldn't surprise me if we found more illegal shit that the Hawks crew were supposed to steer clear of.

With amusement, I watched as Memphis, grumbling under his breath, stomped over to the bar. He picked up some dude by the back of his tee and then threw him over the other side.

"Whoa, man. What the fuck?" the biker complained as he staggered to his feet.

I came up beside Memphis and ordered with a snarl, "Get your shithead of a president out here now."

The guy looked from Memphis to me, and as soon as

his eyes landed on my club's vest, they widened. Memphis wasn't wearing his, but I had mine to prove a point, and the point had been made by the panicked look in the idiot's eyes. He knew I was a part of the original Hawks charter; he also would have noticed the three Hawks embedded into my top left shoulder of the vest, meaning I was third in command.

"S-sure, sure, no worries. I'll go find him." He bolted off quickly.

Memphis turned to the room and shouted, "Wake the fuck up, you dickheads, and clear this place out. Now!"

People were smart enough to listen and stirred back to life. I pulled my phone out and called Talon. He answered with, "Talk."

"Brother, this place is trashed."

"Fuck," he hissed. "You know what to do, and if he doesn't comply, deal. Yeah?"

Chuckling, I replied with, "Yeah." Then snapped my phone shut. Talon meant if Motley wasn't ready to pull his head outta his arse, then he was gone from the club. I smiled at Memphis, who grinned in return. We were happy to be the ones to convey Talon's message, one way or another.

Motley took the hard way. *Stupid dick.* I shook my head as I washed his blood from my hands. He didn't want to run his club the way Talon saw fit; he wanted to trade women and drugs. In the end, he was cut from the charter, and Talon would have to find a new prez. Memphis warned the other members if they didn't like the way Talon ruled, then their arses were gone, as well. Since no one left when the bloodied Motley was kicked out, Memphis sent them to work, cleaning the site up.

While that was happenin', I took Memphis to my mum's. We'd have to stay a couple of extra days to make sure Motley didn't try any shit and the businesses which ran out of the Hawks charter in Caroline Springs weren't under any threat.

We stopped out front of the house I bought my family three years before. It was a five-bedroom, three-bathroom brick joint, with enough room for when I visited. Memphis followed me to the door silently. Without knocking, I walked in and called, "I'm home." Heavy footsteps sounded from within the house, and then Jason was barrelling down the hall.

"Blue!" he yelled. "Blue's here. Mum, Adele, Blue's here." He came to a stop in front of me and smiled big.

I held out my arms and waited for my usual hug, and waited some more. "What, you too old to hug your bro now?" I asked.

"No, yes. I'm nearly eighteen, Blue."

I chuckled. "I know, little man. Doesn't mean you can't hug me." I pulled him into a tight embrace.

"You can't call me little anymore," he said against my

chest. He was right; my brother had shot up. "Hey," he said and pulled out of the hug. "Surprise."

"What do you mean? And listen, this is my mate, Memphis. He's gonna stay a couple of nights with me." I pointed over my shoulder to the silent man taking it all in. I didn't give a shit I was a biker who showed my family love in front of another man, and by the small smile upon Memphis' face, he didn't either.

"Are you gay now?" Jason asked. Memphis barked out a laugh, while I stood gaping like a fucking fish outta water.

"What? No, fuck no."

"Watch your mouth, boy," Adele called from down the end of the hall where the kitchen was.

"Oh," Jason said. "Okay, but come see the surprise. You're gonna love it." He grabbed my wrist and pulled me down the hall. I tried to stop as we passed the sitting room, where I knew my mum would be. She hardly left that room, just sat in there gazing out the window or reading a book. However, when I looked, she wasn't there.

"Hold up, bro. Where's Mum?"

"That's the surprise." He grinned over his shoulder and tugged on my wrist more, so I'd hurry after him down the hall. We reached the kitchen, and Jason let go and walked off to the huge dining table. I entered and went straight to Adele, who was standing at the long, granite-top bench, peeling potatoes. I wrapped my arms around her waist and hugged her.

"How's my old lady?" I asked and kissed her cheek.

"Get your filthy hands off me, boy. I don't know where they've been." She smiled up at me.

"Where's Mum?" I asked, and her smile widened. She gestured with her head to the table off to the left. I looked over and spotted my mum sitting with tears in her eyes, her hands clenched on the table. I stood tall and stiffened. "Mum?" For some reason, it came out as a question. The person at the table looked like my mum, only the woman at the table had life in her eyes.

She nodded. "Hello, my boy."

Holy shit. Holy fucking shit. A shiver ran over my body, my heart jumped to my throat, and I had to clench my jaw to stop the sudden emotions running through me.

Memphis cleared his throat, and then said, "I'll, uh, go get our shit." I nodded but didn't look to see if he'd gone. My eyes were still on my mum.

"How? What... when?" I gulped. Christ, fucking Christ. I was a kick-arse biker, yet I was speechless, stunned. "Fuck," I hissed.

"Language," Adele snapped. "Don't just stand there, boy. Give your momma a hug."

I looked at Adele, and she nodded with a stern gaze. Somehow, it jumpstarted me, and I moved my lead-filled legs. They carried me the distance to get to my mum. She shifted in her seat, her eyes raking over me in a motherly fashion. I stopped in front of her and knelt as her hand reached out to my face and cupped my cheek. I watched her face as tears spilled over and her breath caught before she said, "I'm sorry, my boy. I'm so sorry I wasn't strong enough."

I shook my head. I did not cry; men like me did not cry. But fuck, I felt like it. "No. No one could have been with what you went through," I told her. "How?" I asked again.

"The right medication helped, as well as a new doctor."

She smiled. "You're a handsome young man." She seemed proud, but she hardly knew me. "We—"

"He's not gay," Jason yelled from the other side of the table. "He told me, Mum."

Mum laughed. "That's good to know, though it wouldn't change the love I have for you." She looked at Jason. "For both of you. What I was going to say…." she started, only to pause and hug me. "We have a lot to catch up on."

"Yeah, we do." I grinned as I hugged her tightly.

"I might turn gay," Jason announced.

Mum and I pulled apart, and I asked, "What? Why?"

"Girls suck."

I shook my head as I got from my knees to sit in the

chair next to Mum. I grabbed her hand and held it. "How's that, bro?"

He rolled his eyes. "They keep trying to kiss me."

I burst out laughing. "That's a good thing," I said and looked to Mum, still shocked as shit she was there… back to herself, and sitting next to me.

Beautiful life was back in her eyes.

"Not when I don't want to kiss them."

Adele sighed. I looked over to her and watched the last second of her wiping her eyes. She then pointed a finger at me. "I was afraid of this, you being his brother and good-looking. It had to make him good-looking too, and now all the girls want to stick their tongue in his mouth."

We all laughed, even Jason until he sobered and said, "I'm waiting for the right girl."

"Have you met her, honey?" Mum asked him. He blushed, which meant he thought he had. Damn, even my brother was finding the right one for him.

"Maybe," he mumbled.

"As long as she makes you happy."

He grinned. "She will. She's smart, like me."

I chuckled. "Good. I better go and tell Memphis it's good to come back in. You ladies don't mind him staying?"

"No," Mum smiled up at me as I stood. "I don't mind anything these days. It will be good to know a friend of yours."

Nodding, I bent over and kissed her cheek. "It'll be good to catch up."

She rubbed her hand over my club's vest. "It will be. I'd like to know everything."

"Deal."

CHAPTER SIX

PRESENT

CLARINDA

*T*he phone rang and rang. Panic started to overwhelm me. What would I do if he didn't answer? What did Amy mean by 'a scare'? Who was she talking to? My hands shook as both held the phone to my ear.

"Yellow?" Julian answered sleepily.

"J-Julian," I stuttered. I was cold, so cold. I felt for my bed and sat down, bringing the blanket around my shoulders.

"Clary, honey, what's wrong?" I could hear him shift

in his bed and then a male voice asking him what was going on.

"M-my sister," I whispered. "S-she... I need to leave. Please, please help me. I don't know when it will happen, what she's planning on doing. I have to get out of here." Even with my warm blanket surrounding me, I felt cold to the bone. My body shook without signs of relenting anytime soon. I had no idea if I was going into shock.

"Clarinda, I'm coming. Don't worry, I'm coming. Do you know your address?"

I rattled off my address, and then added, "Julian, y-you have to bring help. She... she'll fight you for me to stay."

"Why?" he asked. "No! Don't tell me yet, buttercup. I'm coming, and I'll bring help. We'll sort everything out. I promise. Do you want to stay on the line with me until I can get to you?"

Blinking back tears of relief, I told him, "No, I better get ready for when you get here."

"Okay, Clary, okay. See you soon, and be careful, honey," he said softly. Before he hung up, I heard him say, "Mattie, baby, get the hell out of bed and ring Talon."

I didn't know how long it would take for Julian to arrive but I wanted to be ready, so I packed what I could into suitcases I knew were in my walk-in closet. It was hard to tell what I packed. I just grabbed anything my hands fell on from my drawers and wardrobe.

I was sure Amy would come running into my room

after I tripped and fell a few times over items I must have dropped. However, she didn't.

It was hard being mostly blind on a normal days. It was worse when I was in a panicked hurry.

At least the packing kept my mind somewhat occupied. But then I heard loud banging on the front door, causing me to jump. With shaking hands, I felt for my bed and the hooded jumper I had placed there earlier. I quickly pulled it over my head as more banging sounded.

"Hang on, Jesus!" my sister yelled from the front of the house, not from my way, where her bedroom was. She must have been in the kitchen. What was she doing up so late, organising my demise?

I walked as fast as I could out of my door and down the hall, my hands glided over the walls in my hurried pace. As I entered the living room, I heard Amy bark, "Who the fuck are you?"

"I'm after Clarinda," a deep voice growled.

"I-I'm here," I said.

"Clary," Julian's voice rang out.

"What the hell are *you* doing here, fag? What's going on?"

"You need to keep your mouth shut, and nothing will fuckin' happen to you. Move back," the man ordered.

I watched her outline move a step back, and in walked two slimmer forms. They both headed my way. "Buttercup," Julian said. He took my hand in his and placed it in another. "This is my fella, Mattie. We're going to get you out of here."

"You're not taking her anywhere," Amy yelled, and a scuffle started in front of us. Mattie, with his hand in mine, moved us back a step. "Get off me. Get *off* me!" Amy screamed.

"Calm the fuck down then. Griz, get Clary's shit. Mattie, you and Julian get her out to the car. Julian stays with her, and you come back to help Griz."

"Got it, boss man," Julian said and started us forward toward the door.

"Rinda… Rinny, what are you doing? Why are you going? You're my sister. Why are you doing this, bringing them into our home?"

"Still," the boss man warned, obviously to my sister.

Letting go of the men beside me, I turned to where my sister's voice had come from. The outline I saw was that of another man pinning her to the floor.

"I thought you were my sister too, but no sister uses them for money. Amy, you were somehow going to scare me into staying? Had you done it before?" I gasped. Of course she had; every time I asked about finding a place of my own. "Oh, God, you have… th-that man the other week? The one who attacked me? Did you get him to do it?"

"What? No, I would never do that."

Lies. What else had she been lying about?

Turning my back on her, I reached my hands out.

Two men I hardly knew were there, ready to take them. To take me away from the nightmare. To take me away from my only family. To safety. How could it be that people I hardly knew were ready to do anything for me, but the one person who should have, didn't?

As soon as I was in an unfamiliar car and Julian hugged me to him, a tidal wave of emotions came crashing down. Julian held me tightly as I tried to find my way out of the water. Though, I didn't know how long it would take me.

While I felt like I was drowning, Julian and Mattie took me to their house. Which—Mattie told me as we walked through the front door—used to be his sister's house, before Talon, who was also known as boss man, moved her in with him. We sat on the couch together, my tears still streamed down my face. My belly twisted and turned in turmoil humiliation and anger. Most of all my heart ached with sadness. I didn't know what I was going to do, where I could go from there. I only knew I wanted... needed to get out of my sister's house.

Although, I had no idea if leaving *was* the right choice, maybe I should have dealt with it on my own, instead of bringing others into my business. Everything was just so hard, and confusing. I wasn't ready to face what the night had brought me.

"Now, Clary. I know you must be going through a lot. Try not to think about it too much now. You need rest, and you can stay here with us for as long as you want. We have two spare rooms," Mattie informed me.

"He's right, buttercup. I've just placed your things in one of the rooms, and you can stay here for as long as you need to."

"Maybe…" I jumped at the new deep, gruff voice. "She should stay at the compound until whatever this is blows over."

"Griz has a point," Mattie said.

Griz? What kind of name was that? For some reason, it had me thinking of Blue and his strange name.

BOOM!

I gripped Mattie as the house shook from some type of explosion out front.

"What the fuck?" Talon growled. "Get her to your room. Stay there until further notice," he barked. I was lifted off the couch into someone's arms as I heard Talon say, "Griz, round up the boys. Let's go." The next thing I heard was the front door being slammed shut.

I was sure it was Mattie who had me, and it was confirmed when he said, "Julian, go lock the front door and run back here." He placed me on a bed. I thought I'd never be as scared as I was at my sister's house, but I was wrong; this new situation was worse. I had no idea what was happening. None of us did. Mattie sat next to me and wrapped an arm around my shoulders. "It's going to be okay. Talon's the president of a motorcycle club, and he's got guys who will help him." He took a breath and yelled, "Julian?"

"I'm here. I'm here." Another door closed, and I assumed it was the one to the bedroom.

CRASH!

Mattie pulled me to the floor and Julian fell on top of us, whispering, "Shit, they've blown out our window."

"Get up. Get the fuck up. The girl comes with us," a harsh voice barked.

I felt Julian's weight disappear, and then Mattie slowly got off my back. Shadows surrounded me. I knew the closest ones were Mattie and Julian, but the other two I didn't.

"You can't take her," Mattie said, his voice shaking slightly. I grabbed his hand. One shadow came at us and hit Mattie in the face, making him fall back. With my hand still in his, I fell on top of him.

"No, please. Please, leave them alone," I begged.

"Clary, no," Julian uttered.

Nothing bothered me but the thought of them getting hurt on my account. I let go of Mattie and shakily got to my feet. "I'll go. I promise... just don't hurt them."

"Move, *now*," the man ordered.

"Clary," Mattie started.

"Don't, please don't. I've caused enough damage." With my arms out in front of me, I wobbled over on unsteady legs toward the window. "I-I can't see. You have to help me," I told my captors. A vise grip wound around my arm just above my elbow, and I was shoved forward and stumbled into another body.

"We meet again, pretty girl."

A weak whimper fell from my lips. It was the man who attacked me in the car weeks before... Henry? He picked me up into his arms. The shadows around me showed we headed toward a window. As he tried to fold me through it, I reached out and scraped my left hand on the jagged glass. Flinching back, I gasped, but then I landed on my feet, stumbling forward as he pushed me the rest of the way and dropped his grip from me.

"Clary, run!" Julian screamed. Noises broke out from within the room behind me. Too scared and frustrated because I couldn't see to help, I did as I was told and started running. My hand shot out in front of me to block my face from anything I couldn't see the outline of. I tripped over something on the ground and fell to my hands and knees, and in the next second, a weight landed on top of me. I struggled blindly to get it off, and whoever it was grunted and swore.

"You stupid bitch, stay still," Henry snapped. He hit me in the side of the head, and my body went sideways. He rolled me to my back and laid on top of me. "You make me hot with all the fighting, sweet girl, but now ain't the time. But before we get rid of you, I'll have my way, and you'll be taking my dick inside you." He thrust his hips forward.

I wanted to throw up, my stomach recoiling from his

scent surrounding me. Tears pooled in my eyes. However, I wasn't ready to give up, and Henry wasn't expecting it either. I reached up and started punching anything above me. He moaned and grunted. "Fuck this, you don't have to look pretty to be gotten rid of." He pushed my hands away and pounded on my face, hit after hit as I tried to fight his hands, his fists, but I didn't know which way they were coming from. He kept changing his movements. A punch to the stomach took my breath away.

This is it. This is how I am going to die.

"Get the fuck off her, now!" a vicious snarl came from somewhere. Henry paused his movements as I tried to fight a breath back into my body. Then, his weight was off me. "Shit. Pick, Stoke, after him now."

Finally, my breath eased in, and I closed my sore eyes. It hurt; everything hurt.

Heat at my side caused me to struggle, to move away. A hand rested on my shoulder. "Shh, easy, it's Talon. Christ, woman, we've got to get you to the hospital."

"No!" I screamed. My eyes went wide. "No, please, they'll find me there. I won't go. I won't."

"S'okay, we'll figure something out."

Relaxing back onto the cold ground, and before I closed my eyes, I asked, "Julian? Mattie?"

"They're fine, but you're not."

"Fuck," someone new hissed. My eyes popped open

again, staring up at the blurry, early-morning sky. "Fuck, fuck, fuck!" the person yelled.

"Griz, calm the hell down. We gotta get her to the compound." Talon gently squeezed my shoulder. "No one will get in there to you, Clarinda," he reassured. I nodded, grimacing with pain.

"She needs a hospital," Griz growled.

"No," both Talon and I said, and then Talon continued with, "Let's get her safe first, and then we'll get Kitten's mum to come look. She used to be a nurse."

They shuffled around me. "Christ, this is gonna hurt her no matter how we do this," Griz said grimly.

"Just do it," I said. All I wanted was to be alone, to be somewhere safe. Then, no one else would be in danger and... I could fall apart once again.

Two strong, large arms slipped under me slowly. I bit my bottom lip to keep my cries of pain at bay.

"Talon?" I heard Julian yell. "Oh God. Oh sweet Jesus. My Clary girl, what did they do?" I felt his hand take mine as Talon walked off at a swift speed with me in his arms... or was it Griz, or someone new? I didn't know. I didn't care as long as I was laid down soon.

"I'll be back," Talon said. I heard his retreating footsteps going the same way Pick and Stoke, whoever they were, had gone.

"Clary?" Julian sobbed.

Breath, just breath through it.

"She's awake, but doesn't want to talk to show us her

pain," Griz said from above me. So it *was* him carrying me, and how did he know?

Doors opened and closed around me, and more heavy footsteps sounded, as well. I kept my eyes shut tightly and held my lips between my teeth. I didn't know where I was, but a scent which was familiar in some way caused me to shout, "Stop!"

"What?" Griz asked.

"What is it, honey?" Julian asked.

Opening my eyes—well, one actually, because the other was swollen shut—I blinked through my permanent haze and made out the outlines. From what it looked like, we were going down a hall, and the space to my left behind my head was where the familiar smell was coming from. I reached out my hand slowly, flinching and gasping when a pain shot through me. "I want to stay in there," I uttered.

"That room ain't free," Griz said.

"Please. Please, I want to stay there. Please." I couldn't be a freak and tell them the scent comforted me.

"He's not here," Julian said. "We can move her when he comes back."

"Fuck, all right."

The door opened. I knew it, not only by the noise but when the scent filled me to the brim. I took a deep breath in, and my body relaxed a bit. Exhaustion took over, and my body eased from its tension.

"Did you see that?" Griz asked as he gently laid me

down. My eyes were closed, and I was too tired and sore to reply.

"What?" Julian asked. His body was behind mine, and something soft lay across me, bringing the wonderful, intoxicating scent with it.

"She took a breath in and her whole body just relaxed."

"She must be comforted by the smell in here."

I was because I knew who that smell belonged to at that point.

Blue.

CHAPTER SEVEN

CLARINDA

*G*asping awake was nothing new. Only that time, it wasn't because of a bad dream; it was because someone had poked a sore spot.

"W-what?" I asked disoriented. My hands slapped out and collided with other, softer hands. "What's going on?"

"It's okay, Clary," Julian said from beside me on the bed. Had he slept the whole time with me? "Mrs. Alexander is checking over your wounds. She's a nurse—"

"Used to be, and call me Nancy," a tender, older woman's voice said. "Now, child, you have a fractured rib and some cuts and bruises on your face. They'll heal in time, but they'll be tender. I'm going to have to wash them."

Licking my dry lips, I asked, "Can't I just have a shower?"

"Of course you can," Nancy said. I felt her move... standing maybe. "Do you want me to help, or should I get my daughter?"

"Your daughter?" *Why would her daughter be here?*

Julian cleared his throat. "That's Zara, Talon's woman. Nancy is also Mattie's mum," he explained.

"I, um, I don't mind who. I would just love a shower, please," I uttered. Julian must have seen my struggle to sit up because he placed one arm around my back and one hand under my arm, slowly helping me rise. I sucked in a jagged breath when it stung. Once I was sitting, I let that breath out through clenched teeth. I found myself again wishing I had proper sight, so I could see the man who clung to my side and the woman whose gentle voice soothed me. I leaned my head back against the wall and sighed. "Maybe I should just go, disappear," I thought out loud.

"No, sweetheart," Nancy said. She must have sat in a chair next to the bed because I heard the sound of the wood giving way under her weight. "You're at your safest here. Come on, take these for the pain while you're sitting up." I felt her hand at mine on the blanket. She placed some pills in it, and then Julian held a cup to my lips as I swallowed down the two tablets.

After I rested my head back against the wall, I tilted it toward Nancy and opened the eye which wasn't swollen shut. "But then I'm bringing trouble to Talon's doorstep. Julian and Mattie's windows have already been broken. God knows what else they'll try."

"It doesn't matter what or if they'll try anything. My son-in-law will keep you safe. He has many men who will also do the same."

Just then, there was loud thumping coming down the hall, and then swearing.

"Hell Mouth, now ain't a good time. She's gettin' checked over," a strange, light male voice said.

"I don't give a fuck what's going on, Pick. I'm going in there, now move."

If I weren't sore, I would have smiled. Hell Mouth. That suited Deanna. I swore that woman wasn't scared of anything or anyone, especially the men around the compound, who I was sure someone had said were bikers.

Did that mean my Blue was a part of a biker club?

There was a knock on the door, and then it opened; my head was already turned that way from talking to Nancy. I saw a larger shadow of someone, presumably Pick.

"All right if Hell Mouth comes in?" he asked.

Julian snorted. "Not like we have a choice."

"I heard that, and no, you don't," Deanna called out from the hall. The manly shadow moved and in came

Deanna's smaller frame. She got to the edge of the bed and hissed, "Fucking hell." I heard her shift; she must have looked back toward the door, because she asked Pick, "Tell me you got these fuckers?"

"No," he growled low, his softer voice turning hard. I saw his form shift to the side of the opened door, the light shining through helping me see three other figures walking into the room.

Julian must have felt me tense. He clutched my hand and squeezed it. "It's okay. It's just Talon, Griz and Zara." I nodded and kept quiet.

"Hello, my gorgeous men," Nancy began from beside us. "We're just about to get our girl in the shower. Can't all this wait until tomorrow, at least?"

"It's already tomorrow, Nance. Sorry, Clary; we need to ask some questions, so we know what we've got to deal with," Talon said.

"O-okay," I whispered. A sniffle at the end of the bed caught my attention. I looked that way, but of course, I couldn't see anything except the silhouette of a female body.

"Hi, I'm Zara." She shifted her arm; she must have waved. "If these guys are too much, just let Deanna or me know. We'll deal with *them*." There was a smile in her voice.

I was used to reading people. I knew from their voices and movements what they were really trying to portray or hide from others. Like Zara, for example. From the way she held her form stiff, I could tell she was worried, and when her shoulders slumped forward, she showed she was sad. And yet, from the smile within her voice, it told me she was nice, caring and concerned. That one still confused me. Why would she be concerned for someone she didn't know?

After returning a small smile, I replied, "Thank you, I will."

"Clarinda, can you tell us what your sister is up to? Why you called Julian in the middle of the night?" Talon asked.

"I overheard my sister on the phone with someone, saying she wanted to give me another scare so I would stay with her. She only wanted me with her because I was useful for the money she received from being my care-giver. I-I panicked." I looked down toward the bed. "There had been a few small accidents I'd been having recently, and I thought it was just me being clumsy, but... now I'm not so sure. Whenever I mentioned I was more than happy to move out, learn to deal with my loss of eyesight on my own, she would get upset with me." I bit my bottom lip to stop the swell of emotions. "N-now, I understand why."

"Is there anything else? Why did you want to leave your sister's house?" Talon asked.

"I-um, I—"

"She was afraid, dipshit. Anyone would have been," Deanna barked.

"Princess," came a warning from Griz. So Deanna was with the bigger, wilder man. I could tell they suited each other.

"Clary, I'm sorry, but the more we know, the easier it is to work out," Talon said.

"No, it's okay." I licked my lips. "Deanna's right. I was afraid. You see, my sister was acting strangely that afternoon. She was angry about something and took it out on me when I wasn't out front to meet her at the library. She had to come in and get me—"

Deanna scoffed. "Yeah, I'd call hitting her in the back of the head a few times 'not happy'. She's a bitch." She moved from the side of the bed next to Nancy and paced behind Zara's form. "You should have just come with us then. This wouldn't have happened; you wouldn't be hurt," she mumbled to herself.

"It's hard to know who to trust or what to do when you're like this," I said, pointing to my eyes. "And really, anyone would think they could trust their own sister. Obviously not." I pounded my fist on the bed. "Shit, fuck, what did I ever do to her? Nothing. Well, I suppose I've been a burden after becoming like this, after witnessing our parents die in that fucking fire. All I did was care. All I ever do is manage to be in the wrong situation at the wrong time. And now look at me." I pounded my chest. *Dammit, that hurt.* "I'm in a bed, in a place with people I hardly know, because of my fucked-up sister and situation. Why me? Why do I deserve this? What does that bitch want from me?" Suddenly, I stopped. My chest rose and fell with speed as I tried to keep it all together.

"Lemon cake, it's about time you cracked," Julian said seriously. No wonder people loved him; everyone needed to have a Julian around in tense moments.

I snorted out a deranged laugh. "Obviously, I just needed a little bit of time."

"Talon, honey?" Zara said quietly.

"Right," Talon growled. "Clary, you're to stay here. We'll find out what we can, but no matter what you do, do not contact your sister or go near her."

"It's certain she's doing this shit for another reason. It can't be just for the caregiver money," Griz added.

I nodded; that thought had also crossed my mind, as well. However, what I wanted to know was what else she could want from me.

"Griz, let's hit it. Clary, get some rest, sweetheart," Talon said. He moved toward Zara, and their forms melded together. Movement on Julian's side of the bed caught my attention; it was Griz. He touched my shoulder gently and said, "Rest easy, darlin'. We'll figure it all out." My eyes filled with tears.

"Griz," Deanna snapped, "you can't be sweet. She'll burst like a dam and blubber tears out everywhere. I can't handle that shit, baby; you know that. So get the fuck out."

I choked on a laugh. Deanna was definitely a straight shooter.

"Damn lucky I love you, woman," Griz growled. I heard a slap and Deanna swore. I smirked because I knew she'd just been slapped on the arse.

"Later, Boss Man and Boo-Boo," Julian called.

"Julian, no fucking way. You ever call me that again, we're gonna have a problem," Griz barked from the door before it slammed closed.

"Shoot, I liked that one," Julian said. I could hear the pout in his voice.

Deanna, Zara, and Nancy laughed. "Where did you get that one from?" Nancy asked.

"You know, Yogi Bear and Boo-Boo."

"You should have tried for Yogi Bear first," I suggested.

"Yeah, I didn't think of that. I loved Boo-Boo for him." He sighed.

"I'd even hurt you if you called *me* that," Deanna said.

"Okay, folks," Nancy started, the creaks in the chair signalling that she stood. "Let's get Clary organised so she can get some rest."

"Well, sorry, Clary, but I can't help with that," Deanna said. "You're pretty and all, but I'm not ready to see you naked."

Nancy scoffed. "Come on, child. I'll help you to the bathroom and get you in the shower. Zara, do you have some loose, comfortable clothes she can get changed into?"

"I'm sure I do in Talon's room. I'll be back soon." She started for the door.

"Hang on; I'll come. Someone needs to light a fire under the guys' arses to get this figured out," Deanna said.

"Wait," I called. "Thank you. All of you."

"Oh, hummingbird, it's our pleasure to help you. Now, you go for a shower, and I'll change the sheets."

I wanted to tell him not to because I still wanted the sweet smell of Blue on the sheets. My heart thudded behind my ribs.

Blue.

I was in his room.

Still, I kept quiet; I didn't want to sound like a fool. Besides, maybe it wasn't his room anyway. Maybe it just smelled like the man from my dreams.

THREE DAYS LATER, I found out it was indeed Blue's room I was staying in, and what told me was the hurricane form of Ivy Morrison. I'd been pampered for those three days. If it wasn't Julian fawning over me by feeding me, talking with me or keeping me company, it was Zara, Deanna or Nancy. Until the day they were all busy, and Ivy walked into the room while I was listening to the news on the television.

The door opened, and then it started. "Hi, you must

be Clarinda. Beautiful name, by the way. I'm Ivy Morrison. I own a café not far from here. You should come by sometime. Anyway, how I came about being here is because I'm Killer's woman…or so I've been told. Though, I don't call him Killer. He's Fox to me. It would be weird calling my man Killer." She giggled as she sat in the chair next to the bed. "I thought I'd come and introduce myself. I'm still getting to know everyone here as well, so I know sometimes it can be a little overwhelming, especially after something so terrible has happened. I went through my own personal Hell. You see, I started out on a dating site. That's where I met Fox; he lost a bet, and they put him on the site." She sighed a happy, content sigh at the thought.

"However, not only Fox messaged me about a date. In the end, long story short, I ended up getting a stalker of sorts. He came after me, and all Hell broke loose. It finished with him going to jail, and I now have a scar across my neck where he tried to slice my throat open." I gasped. "Oh, don't worry. Fox made sure he got payback for it. Everything is good now. Fox is the best." She took a breath.

"Hey, do you know this is Blue's room? I wonder why they put you in here. He's away at the moment, seeing his mum. He didn't go beforehand because he stayed to help me and my situation. Nice guy, though." She laughed. "Very good-looking. A lot of these bikers *are* handsome, and sometimes I get flustered and talk and talk without thinking about what I'm saying…oh, God, kind of like I am now. Sorry, I have a habit of doing it when I'm nervous, too."

Smiling at her, I asked, "Why are you nervous?"

"I get nervous when I meet new people. But they said I could come in here and meet you while Fox is in a meeting with his biker brothers. I hope you don't mind."

"Not at all." After all, she'd given me the answer I was too worried to ask. It was, after all, *my* Blue's room I was staying in. There could only be one Blue, right? That name wasn't a regular name, like Joe or Harry. It had to be *my* Blue.

Suddenly, anticipation took over my body and I felt giddy. I was looking forward to seeing Blue when he got back.

I just hoped he would be happy to see me.

"Do you want to play a game?" Ivy asked.

"Um…I'm not sure if anyone has mentioned I don't have full sight."

"Really? Oh, no, they didn't, or I wouldn't have said anything. Now I feel like a tool asking to play a game. Though, I could probably think of a game to play without using our eyes. How did that happen anyway? Oh, my God, sorry; I shouldn't have asked. See? I can be really inappropriate sometimes, too."

While I laughed, I just knew I was going to get along wonderfully with Ivy. I knew because I found myself telling her all about my horrid past.

CHAPTER EIGHT

BLUE

a few days away turned into a week and a half. However, it felt longer, way longer. While I bloody enjoyed my time getting to know my mum again, I also enjoyed the home-cooked meals from Adele and even Jason annoying the hell outta me when he asked question after question.

Though, I didn't only stay for my family, but also to get the Caroline Springs Hawks charter under control. The place not only looked a fucking mess on the outside, but it was chaotic on the inside, as well. The books were up the shit. We had spread the word through town that Motley was no longer in charge, and until Talon could find another president, Memphis was taking over the roll.

Ah, Memphis. He was a fucking surprise. I kinda regretted not spending more time with the dude. Since I'd been around him in a one-on-one situation, especially at the compound organising shit, I learned there was more to him than what he showed back home. Not only was he a good brother to the club, I learned he had the smarts to be a leader, and I was going to suggest to Talon when I got home that we should make the change for Memphis to become President of the Hawks charter in Caroline Springs more permanent.

He was ruthless when he needed to be, mean, funny and compassionate. The funny and compassionate part I saw more when he joined us for dinner at home, or when he was just hangin' in the living room, or even spending time with Jason.

The only thing that freaked the crap outta me was the way him and my mum got… cosy with each other. Little looks here, little touches there when he'd help her from a chair or something, or when she'd be cooking, and he'd offer to help. I noticed she'd get close to him, touch his arm to get his attention.

So then, when Memphis came to me before I left and asked for my blessing to see if my mum would be interested in going out on a date, it didn't shock me. It was awkward as hell, but I was never shocked.

Of course, I threatened his arse to take care of her. I

wouldn't be the proper son if I didn't. He took it in stride and swore on his life that he would.

I already knew he would, and the thought of leaving Memphis in Caroline Springs with my family—because mum offered him to stay at her house instead of the compound—eased some of the tension I had been feeling about leaving.

Jason was pissed I had to go, but I couldn't stay in a place which no longer felt like home to me. My home was with my brothers. I suggested to him that when he turned twenty-one, if he was interested, he could think of joining Hawks, but he'd have to come to Ballarat to do it. He'd been so fucking happy I'd even suggested it.

However, the tension built inside of me had eased a bit knowing Memphis was there, steppin' up to take on the care of my family, 'cause he was hot for Mum —*shudder*. Yet, the guilt I felt for leaving was still there, which was why I knew I'd be making more trips down to see them, even after I expressed that to Mum one night and she told me I should never feel guilty. She said I had taken on more than what any other son would have, and it was my time to live free with less stress. It was all worth it. That's what family did; they took care of each other.

Riding my baby home with the words from my mum helped settle some of the guilt. In my eyes, every goddamn man should have a bike, to feel the thrill of the power between your legs, to know you're in control of such a big beast.

Damn, all this emotional shit. While I get my arse waxed, maybe I should look into getting my balls done, as well.

Pulling into the compound's car park, I had a smile on my face, it felt great to be back. Being late afternoon, some brothers were working out front of the mechanical area on some cars. I sent them a chin lift and then walked through the front door. As I kept going, I heard voices in the main common area. Through the doorway, I spotted Talon with Griz, Stoke, Killer, and Pick around the bar talking.

"Hey, brothers. What's goin' on?" I asked, making my way over to them. They all turned as soon as I spoke, and I knew straight away from their severe expressions that something was up.

"S'up, Blue?" Talon asked.

"Spill the shit. What's going down now, and why haven't I been told?" I demanded as I came to a stop beside Talon and Killer.

"He's gonna find out as soon as he walks through his door here anyway," Stoke chuckled.

"What'ya mean?" Was someone in my room? Who the fuck could it be? Holy fucking shit, had I knocked someone up? I hoped to Christ not. All the bitches I'd been with were just that—bitches. While the pansies stood and eyed each other on how to start, I stalked off and headed to my room.

"Blue, wait the fuck up," Talon called. His footsteps were fast approaching.

"Brother," Killer warned on a growl. *WTF?* "You go in gentle. You'll scare her otherwise."

Again, what the fucking fuck?

In the hall to the rooms, I spotted Billy sitting on the floor outside *my* room. He saw me, must have seen the damn annoyed, pissed state I was in and quickly stood, holding his hands out. "Blue, she's sleeping. You go in there all gung-ho and you'll scare the fuck outta her. She don't know you."

"Not sure of that," Griz uttered under his breath.

Ignoring it, because I was confused as fuck and getting more pissed, I yelled, "Then what is she—whoever the fuck *she* is—doing in my room?"

Suddenly, my door opened abruptly and Ivy filled the doorway, glaring at us. "Will you guys keep it down? She's healing really well, but it's only been a few days, so she still needs her rest." She started to eye my brothers with annoyance, but then her eyes landed on me. "Oh, hey, Blue. Damn, will you want your room back? I'd hate to wake her up. She overdid it today with walking around here; her ribs were hurting her. But I'm sure she'd move if she knew the person the room belongs to is back."

"Billy, you get back to work and help lock up. We've got it here," Talon ordered.

"Sure, boss," he said, and ran off down the hall.

"Someone please tell me what in Christ is going on?" I hissed through clenched teeth.

Ivy stepped out of my room and shut the door behind her. She motioned with her hands at the men around her. "Come on, fill the poor guy in."

"Precious." Killer smirked at his woman while shaking his head, and then he turned to me and shocked the fuck out of me. "Julian's new friend had a situation. Her sister was using her for money she got for taking care of her. The woman found out when she overheard a convo between her sister and some guy, saying she needed another scare to stick around so they'd keep getting the money. She rang Julian. Talon and Griz went over with him and got her out. They took her to Wildcat's old house. That's when shit blew up. Literally. They sparked a car out front, and while Talon and Griz checked it out, they got into the house and took her, beat her before Talon could get to her. She's roughed up and scared. Still, there's a tough side to her. No one has heard her complain, even after everything she's gone through."

Griz cleared his throat. "The women have taken her under their wings. She a part of them now, so she's a part of us, which is why she's staying here at the compound until we get some fuckin' answers."

"Why in my room though?"

"That's the funny thing. I was carrying her down this hall and she yelled at me to stop. She wanted to stay in there." He thumbed to my door. "She wouldn't take no for an answer, and when I took her in, it was like her whole body relaxed. This is gonna sound strange as shit, but I think she knew your scent. She took in a breath and her body sagged in my arms."

"What's her name? No one's said it once."

"Clarinda," Talon said.

My eyes widened. My heart stopped. It couldn't be, but how many Clarinda's were out there? No, fuck no. Someone beat her, touched her in ways she didn't want. My fists clenched. My jaw tightened as I tried to rein the anger back in.

Motherfucking Christ.

"It's hitting him and hard," Stoke snapped.

Hands grabbed my arms.

"You need to cool it, brother," Killer growled.

After deep breaths through my nose, I then said, "I'm fine. I'm good. Let me go." Griz and Killer stepped away from me. "When did this happen?"

"So you know her?" Talon asked.

My eyes snapped to him. I knew they were wild because I sure as fuck knew I didn't like the thought of anyone hurting my Clary. "Yeah, I do, but I'll explain later. When did this happen?" I clipped.

"Last Friday," Talon answered.

"Why didn't anyone tell me? Why wasn't I informed something was going down?"

"You had other shit goin' on. We dealt with it. *If we*

knew you knew her, we would have contacted you straight away."

I sighed. "I only met her a couple of times, but fuck, she made an impression. Still, there was confusion going on between us, mix-ups and shit. The last time I saw her was fucked up. Henry, one of the local drugos, was attacking her. I stopped it." Shaking my head, I added, "I let her leave with her bitch of a sister. I shouldn't have. I knew something was going on with her; I could see it in her. I shouldn't have fuckin' let her leave."

"Don't take that one on, Blue," Ivy whispered. "I've gotten to know Clary over the last couple of days, and I know she wouldn't have listened to you. Back then, she believed her sister would keep her safe not set her up."

I nodded. It was fine for Ivy to say that, but it still didn't help the regret beating through me right then.

Standing straighter, I said, "I'm going in to grab some shit. I'll get another room here. If that's where Clary wants to stay, then she stays."

"After you've done that, come to the office and we'll talk more. Tell you what we've found, yeah?" Talon asked.

I gave him a chin lift, and my brothers started off. Killer waited for Ivy as she stepped up beside me, placed her hand on my arm and uttered, "She's going to be fine, Blue. I know you didn't listen to me before, but none of this was your fault. It would be ridiculous if you keep thinking it."

"Cupcake," Killer warned.

I watched her roll her eyes at her man and look at me. "I think she knew this was your room, too. She feels safe in there, and I know you'll keep her thinking it." With that, she squeezed my arm and went to her man, who curled his arm around her shoulders as they walked off whispering. I just bet Killer was warning her bikers didn't like to be told they were being ridiculous because we sure as fuck didn't. Luckily for Ivy, she could get away with it.

The only light in the room when I opened the door was coming from my TV attached to the wall on the right side of the room. I closed the door behind me, and the room fell darker. My eyes landed on the beautiful sleeping form of Clary on my bed. I couldn't help myself; I crept closer to take all of her in. She was tucked tightly under the blanket on her back, and I could make out that her eye was bruised, her lips were cut, and she had small scratches on her face.

Fuck! My fist clenched once again. I breathed deeply through my nose.

Why did this have to happen to her?

Jesus. Life was so fuckin' unfair to people who didn't deserve its crap.

Shaking my head, I turned my back on her and went to my walk-in closet bedside my TV. I rummaged through my shit, found a duffle bag and piled clothes into it. I was gonna find a room close to her. No one was gonna touch her again.

Back out in the room, I went to my drawers beside

the bed on the far side, away from the door. As I slid one open, the bed shifted. My eyes went there straight away. She'd turned toward me. I quickly grabbed some boxers and shoved them in my bag. When I closed the drawer, I looked back down to Clary to find her eyes open and on me. Her brows were down; she seemed confused, but then she took in a deep breath, gasped and uttered, "Blue?"

How in the fuck did she know I was there when she couldn't see?

"Hey, sugar," I said and knelt down beside the bed. Her eyes followed me. I had no idea how she was able to track me. "I heard you've been up to no good."

Her bottom lip trembled, and she scoffed weakly. "You could say that." That was when she burst out crying.

Shit. Motherfuckers making her cry... or had it been because of me?

All I knew was my whole being wanted to comfort her. I climbed onto the bed and gently drew her to me so her back rested against my chest and my arms wound around her waist. "Shh, baby. It'll be okay. It's gonna be fine." I really didn't know what to say. She shifted, her hands gripped tightly onto my arms as she nuzzled her head into my neck. "You've come to the right place for help, sugar. They've all taken to you. Everyone's willing to help."

She sniffed and uttered, "I-I'm sorry." She tried to pull away, but I held her close.

"You've got nothing to apologise for, Clary. Nothing. From what I know, this shit has happened *to* you. You caused none of it."

How was this beautiful woman allowin' me to comfort her?

There was a knock at the door and Clary cringed in my arms, which was how I knew she didn't want to see anyone.

"Whoever it is, go the fuck away," I called.

I wanted nothing to break the moment. Clary was allowin' *me*—a damned moody biker she hardly knew—to hold her after her ordeal. I just wished I was fuckin' there for her when everything happened. I wished I'd fought harder to get in contact with her, but I'd suspected then she didn't really want to. I also fuckin' wished I'd stole her away that day, even though I knew she had troubles.

Most of all, I wished I was the man for her.

But I knew I wasn't. She deserved more than me.

All I could give her was the moment.

CHAPTER NINE

CLARINDA

*W*hoever had been at the door must have left. The room fell silent as Blue obviously ran through some thoughts in his mind. I didn't mean to break down. When I woke and found the scent of him was so intense I just knew he was in the room. At first, I thought I had been dreaming when I saw an outline of someone standing in front of me. Then I called out to him, and his sweet, intoxicating voice spoke back. Emotions overwhelmed me. *He's here. My Blue, my saviour, is here in front of me.*

When he brought me into his arms, I had never felt so cherished. It was apparent someone had told him what had happened, and he was kind enough to show me he cared.

I wanted to stay in his arms forever, though I knew that wasn't going to be possible. Yes, he was showing me comfort, but his form was stiff. I wasn't sure if he actually wanted to be there. I probably freaked him out by how I reacted. Maybe not many women cried in front of him, and he didn't know what to do, but what he was doing was enough. It was perfect.

However, there was something else. From what I could sense, he was worried but standoffish, which caused me to think he didn't really want to be here in the room with me.

His room.

God, would he even be in here if it wasn't his room?

Probably not.

I shifted away from him. At first, he fought it and held me tighter, until he let me go. I turned so he could see my face and I could see the blurred outline of his. "I'm sorry for intruding on your personal space, Blue. I'll get my things and move." I placed my palms on the bed and went to shift forward, only to stop when he put his hand on my arm.

"I'd feel better if you stayed here. There's plenty of space in this place. I'll go stay in another room."

Why would he give up his room for me?

I didn't know what to make of his kind gesture. I felt stupid, yet relieved. Stupid for allowing my emotions to take control and attach them to a man I hardly knew and relieved he wouldn't move me from a room which had me feeling like it was a home to me.

Annoyance was also present because, for the first time in a long time, I felt something for a man I had never felt... lust, desire, even though I didn't know him.

Though, I knew I wanted to get to know him. I *wanted* him.

Could a man like Blue ever want anything from me?

"I-I can't have you doing that. It's your room."

"Please...for me, stay in here." He gently tucked my wayward hair behind my ear. Oh, God, what did I look like? Terrible, I was sure. His finger glided over my cheek. "Clary... can I ask how this happened? You can't see anything, right?"

I bit my bottom lip, and with no thought at all, I rested my back against his chest and told him the story of my parents, the fire, everything. All that time, he remained silent and listened. When I came to the part of my parents' death, his arms convulsed around me, warming me to the bone because it showed he was truly listening and he hated that for me. He hated what I had been through, what I had witnessed.

"So that's how you came to live with your sister?" he asked.

I nodded, suddenly tired from my storytelling. "She was at the hospital that night, and when I woke the next day, she took me into her care and home with her."

"Where was she the night of the fire?"

Leaning forward, I turned to face him. I was too tired to talk of my past because a sudden thought crossed my mind and I wanted to fulfil it. "Out at some party," I said distractedly. I called up enough courage to ask, "Can... can I, um... touch you?" He hissed in a quick breath. When he stayed silent, I took that as a yes and with shaky fingers, I reached one hand up. From the shadow I saw of his outline, I could see the direction I needed to go. I jumped when my fingers touched the rough stubble on his chin, which caused Blue also to jump. My hand quickly retreated. "Sorry, I shouldn't have—"

"No," he started and grabbed my hand in his, slowly pulling my hand toward him again. That time, when the roughness surprised me, I didn't jump. "See? It's fine. I need a shave, actually, but I've been away, busy."

His hand left mine, and by the sound, I could tell he'd placed it back on the bed. I ran my fingers over his chin, his neck and then back up to his cheek, over to his temple and forehead. Reaching up with my other hand, I placed it on the other side of his face. My fingers sorted out every bump and groove. I closed my eyes, trying to picture and memorise what he looked like, what he felt like.

In some ways, on some days, I got the feeling of gladness. Glad I was mostly blind because it meant my other senses were stronger.

"I should have tried harder to contact you," Blue said quietly.

I shook my head. "I shouldn't have listened to my sister when she said you hadn't called."

Both of our breaths mingled with each other's; we were that close. All I knew was I liked everything I felt. He bounced on the bed when I asked, "What colour eyes do you have?"

"Blue," he replied, his voice lowered and thick.

"And hair?" I asked as I ran my fingers through his longer, smooth locks.

"Blond."

I smiled. I could just about picture him, but there was one place which was blank, one place my fingers had yet to discover.

His lips.

As if he knew I was hesitating, his hand gripped mine once more and dragged them out of his hair. He let go for a second to take only two fingers in his hand, and then he went painstakingly slow as he guided the hand which held my shaking fingers down to his lips. After he knew I wasn't going to withdraw, and after he laid a gentle kiss on my fingertips, he let go of my hand. My fingers stayed there and ran tenderly over his plush, succulent lips, first the bottom one then the top.

As I licked my dry lips, he groaned and asked around my fingers, "Is it my turn now?"

Through my confusion, I questioned, "Pardon?"

He took my hand from his lips and placed it on the bed, where my other hand was. Then, gently, he ran his hand from mine, up my arm, to my shoulder and then my neck. My body shivered from his touch; it was warm, yet rough from his hardworking hands. It thrilled me he was touching me like that. He circled my ear and tucked my hair behind it. Then, slowly, as if he was waiting for me to say stop or something, he ran a finger to my cheek. From there, he went up to my forehead as his other hand threaded through my hair. His finger on my face didn't stop. It slid down my forehead to my nose, where he tapped once. I smiled; he moaned.

"I want to feel your lips," he growled. He was closer; I could feel his breath blowing across my cheek as he added, "But not with my fingers… with my lips. Would you let that happen, sugar?" I hummed my approval; my heart beat wildly in my chest, and I was surprised he couldn't hear it. Then, all thought fled my body as his lips softly touched mine.

I gasped and pulled back. "Ow." My fingers went to my lip which was still healing. I had forgotten all about it at the moment.

"Shit. Fuck, sorry. Are you okay?" I felt the air move beside my head, and I knew he was reaching out to me. I waited for that touch, but it never came. Instead, he climbed from the bed.

"Wait," I said and reached out blindly, trying to grab any part of him to stop him. The bad part was my hand collided with his penis, and before I knew what it was, my hand clenched around the large, *firm* cock. Gasping, it was my turn to apologise, "Oh, God, I'm sorry. I-I didn't know." I waved in his general area. "Sorry."

He chuckled, but it was strained. "Don't worry about it, really. But, ah, I better go. You know, get a room and uh, have a shower—from the ride—hell, I mean the ride on my Harley. I just got back not that long ago...."

He was flustered. Blue Skies was flustered.

"You don't have to go. I um... won't feel you up again."

He groaned and moved from the side of the bed toward the door. "I do. I have some shit to take care of. I'll, uh, catch ya later." With that, he opened the door and walked out, quickly closing it behind him. All the sounds of Blue leaving suddenly pained me. I wanted him to stay. I wanted him like I had never wanted another man.

Why did that biker have such a strong pull over me and my feelings?

And why did he leave in such a hurry? He was the one who wanted to kiss me. That was wrong; I also wanted to kiss him, but he made a move, and then he just about ran from the room.

I was frustrated, mentally and sexually.

Then again, maybe he thought I'd be a burden on him, as well... just like my own sister did.

What I needed to do was learn to live for just me, learn to depend on me alone, and that had to start immediately. It was time to get my own room. Having Blue's scent filling my senses confused me, maybe even into thinking I felt more for him than I should. Maybe I was just infatuated with him because he had shown me I was more than just a nuisance blind girl.

But I couldn't do that. Could I? Could I be on my own?

Yes, I had to stand on my own two feet.

I swept the bedspread out of my way and slowly climbed out of bed. I had to find someone in charge. Hopefully, I would run into Talon or Zara, and ask them if I could switch rooms. Then I could see if what I was feeling for Blue was biased because he surrounded me from being in his area.

With my decision made, I felt clearer, and I felt great for it. I needed to get back to that independent woman I was before anything ever happened. I opened the door and stepped out. The air was cooler out in the hall, and that was when I realised I was in boy-shorts and a cami. It was too late to go back. I knew I was safe there, so I walked down the hall with my hands on each wall, guiding my way. I just hoped I was heading in the right direction.

I knew I was when I heard voices growing louder. I was either walking toward a room full of people, or they were heading my way. Abruptly, the voices stopped when my hands reached the curve at the end of the hallway, announcing I had entered another, brighter room. I squinted from the sudden light hitting my eyes.

Not knowing where I had to go, I called out, "Um, excuse me, but can someone help me please?"

Chairs got pushed back, scuffing noises reached my ears, and suddenly, a lot of loud, stomping footsteps approached my way.

"Don't you fuckin' dare," I heard Blue snarl.

The room fell eerily quiet, and then men swore or mumbled about something. I couldn't make out what it was, and when warm, familiar hands and a familiar scent reached my nose, I didn't care what the other men were going on about.

"Clary, what in the hell are you doing?" he snapped.

"W-what do you mean?" I wasn't doing anything which granted the pissed tone in his voice. In fact, it annoyed me. I shrugged out of his hands which were on my arms and took a step back, only my back hit a wall. My brows furrowed in confusion. I hadn't moved that far from the hall, so why was I suddenly against a wall?

"Whoa, sweetheart," the wall behind me said with a smile in his voice, and then vise-like arms wound around my waist. "Although, I don't mind being walked into."

"Dodge, hands off and step the fuck back, *now*," Blue snarled.

"Blue," said a new voice, and because the room was so bright, I saw the new figure step up beside Blue in front of me. Not only from the deep voice, but from the build of the shadow, I knew who it was.

"Talon, just the man I wanted to see," I said and tried

to step out of the grabby arms, but they tightened, so I got nowhere.

"Why you wanna see him?" Blue questioned. "Dodge, if you don't let go, you're gonna be on the fuckin' floor in the next second."

Dodge chuckled. "I'd like to see you try, brother."

From hearing conversations in the past so many days, I knew they weren't real brothers, but biker ones. It also helped that Zara had explained parts about living with bikers.

"Dodge," Talon warned.

"Damn, boss, you're no fun." His hand slowly slipped from my waist to my hips, and then I felt a tap on my bum which caused me to gasp. "Any time you wanna party, you let me know, sweetheart. I *will* rock your world. Not like Blue here, it'll be way better."

Shocked by his words and without thinking, because I was damned *shocked,* I nodded mutely. He laughed, and a growl came from in front of me.

"Christ, why are you nodding?" Blue asked ghastly.

"I... no, I'm not—I wouldn't... I didn't...." Growling under my breath, I chose to ignore the question after I couldn't find words to answer it. "Talon, can I talk to you for a moment? Unless Zara is around? Or Deanna?"

"Ah, the women ain't here." Why did he sound amused?

"Why. Do. You. Wanna. Talk. To. Him?" Blue queried

slowly through clenched teeth. At least, it sounded like it, as though he was holding back his anger.

"Brother," Talon said. I saw movement, and all I could put it down to was that Talon was waving his arm out in front of him. "You wanna deal with that before all hell breaks out?"

Was... no, he couldn't be. But was he gesturing toward me? I wasn't sure, but I glared anyway. Blue was shifting about and mumbling under his breath.

"What do you mean 'deal with that', Talon? Do you mean me? I don't need to be dealt with. I'm fine at taking care of myself. In fact, I—"

"Shut it, Clary," Blue bit out from in front of me, and then in the next second, something was slipped over my head and Blue's scent was the strongest it had ever been.

"W-what are you doing?" I asked as he guided my arms through the holes of, obviously, his tee.

"I didn't see it in the bedroom because it was darker. Sugar, your top is see-through, and you're not wearing anything under it."

No!

Oh my God. I paled, absolutley horrified.

"I-I didn't know," I stuttered in a small voice.

CHAPTER TEN

BLUE

*C*hrist. *Motherfucking shit.* I wanted to stay pissed at her. I really wanted to. I mean, come the fuck on. She walked into a roomful of men wearing short-shorts and a top which showed her round, perky breasts. And it was a fucking roomful of bikers for that damned matter, and then, in her sweet voice, she asked for help. My brothers nearly ripped each other apart to get to her.

That was when I saw red. I even knocked some brothers out of the way to get to her first, and then fucking Dodge came out of nowhere and placed his hands on what was goddamn *mine*. Shit, I was prepared to fight the fucker, and everyone knew what a mean, dirty fighter that guy was.

However, I couldn't stay mad long, not when she looked up at me with doe-eyes and stuttered that she didn't know. Of course she wouldn't. What I wanted to know was who gave her those clothes in the first place. I was gonna have a word with that person.

I placed my hands on her upper arms and rubbed up and down. "I know, sugar. I know." I turned my head to Talon; he grinned like a fucking fool. "Mine," I stated with a glare in my eyes. He knew what I was getting at, and from the confused look on Clary's face, she didn't have a clue. Which was good.

I was being a selfish bastard, but I knew as soon as I stepped out of my bedroom with a stiff dick and a hard yet sweet beat in my chest that I was gonna prepare myself to be everything I needed to be for her. Walking out of that room was the hardest thing I'd ever done. Walking out that door, away from her, changed so much in me. I knew I'd never want to do it again. I could only hope she would let me in her mind, in her arms, soul, heart, and bed.

"Sure, Blue," he chuckled.

"Make it clear to everyone," I said.

"My guess is they already know."

"Good," I uttered as I looked down at Clary's face. Even though it was bruised, it was the prettiest one I'd ever laid eyes on. My dick twitched in my jeans, though it'd have to wait to get what it wanted; Clary's safety and care came first. I had to win her over. I had to lay every-

thing on the table and tell her what I wanted from her...
but that would all have to wait until her crap was over,
and only then would I find out if I had a chance.

Watching her, there was no way in Hell I could *not* be
a selfish bastard and take a chance on her... us. If she
wanted it also.

Jesus. I hoped she'd want it.

"Now, what did you want to talk to Talon about?" I
asked. Talon stepped closer. I glared at him, and then he
burst out laughing.

Once he caught a breath, he said, "Finally, brother,
you get it."

"Whatever," I grumbled because he was right. I did get
it. I understood why he was so possessive of Zara. Fuck, I
also regretted trying to get her attention. I couldn't blame
the guy for not being his usual self with me for a few
months. I would've had a shit haemorrhage if the shoe
was on the other foot. "Clary?" I said and waited for her
answer.

"Oh, I wanted to change rooms."

"What?" I hissed.

"Clarinda," Talon started before I could even breathe
fire down her neck. "Not gonna happen, babe. You're
staying in Blue's room."

"But—"

"No, sugar. You're staying in there and that's final," I
ordered as Talon groaned loudly beside me. I watched as

he hit his hand against his forehead and shook his head at me.

"That's final?" Clary snapped. "Really, Blue? Really?" she yelled. My dick throbbed once again. I kinda liked seeing her cranky.

"Shit, brother. I'm leaving you to this. My advice: don't do that shit again, and get her into a more private room before she hands you your balls."

That was a good fucking idea because, from the scowl upon her cute face, she was about to take my nuts to her hand. Not that I'd mind; only that time, I had a feeling she'd squeeze the shit outta them instead of caressing them like I wanted her to.

Stepping up to her so she could feel my front pressed against hers, I bent slightly, placed my hands on her arse then hoisted her up. She automatically wrapped her legs around my waist and her arms around my neck.

"What are you doing?" she gasped.

I walked down the hall before I answered with, "I really don't want to be yelled at in front of my brothers, sugar. So, we're going to our room to do it."

Jesus. Had she noticed the slip up when I said *our* room? It was hard to tell because her body was still tense; I could feel it as I held her against me… as her warm, sweet spot rubbed against my boner. Damn, I wanted to bring her in tighter against it. I wanted to pull the flimsy shirts and panties aside and sink my cock into her pussy.

I didn't. Of fuckin' course I didn't. I wasn't some goddamned animal who couldn't help his urges.

At least, most of the time.

The bedroom door was already open, so I walked straight in. I placed her fantastic arse on my bed, turned around and went over to shut the door.

"Let me have it," I said and leaned against the door with my arms across my chest.

She sighed. "Come away from the door so I can punch you then." At least the smirk on her lips told me she was playing with me at least a little.

"Hang on. How did you know I was leaning against the door... and when I first came in the room, how did you know it was me?" I questioned her. It was something I wanted to ask from the start.

From the glare of the TV still being on, I could make out the traces of a blush forming on her cheeks. Why would she be blushing? It was sure as shit cute on her. I made my way over to her side and sat. "How, Clary?"

She licked her lips, and hell, I wanted to follow her tongue with my own, but then she said, "I'm not one hundred percent blind. I can see shadowing, outlines of things and people if they're close and the room is bright."

"But it wasn't bright when I came in earlier. You woke up and said my name."

"Um, being blind has helped my other senses become stronger."

"Woman," I growled out. "Get to the point."

"I smelled you, okay? Your scents strong."

Still, I was puzzled. "How did you know my... scent?"

Her blush was back before she uttered, "In the café that day, it filled the room and I... I guess I remembered it."

Christ. I liked that. I liked it a lot because it meant she had taken notice.

I reckoned I had a chance with Clarinda... *fuck*, what was her last name?

"What's your last name, sugar?"

"James." She took a breath and asked, "Can we get back to how you *told* me I was staying in here, and that it was *final*?"

Snorting, I leaned forward and placed my elbows on my thighs. "Sorry about that. But I was fuckin' pissed that nearly every brother got to see you like...." I growled low. "I was pissed, okay? Why did you want to move rooms?" I asked to the floor.

She squirmed beside me, so I took a look at her, and I saw another blush. Now, that just made me fucking curious.

"I didn't want to be a burden."

Studying her, I knew she'd lied; she turned her face from my direction and looked elsewhere. I sat up straight and with my hand under her chin I turned her head toward me. "I don't think that's it at all, Clary."

She shoved my hand away and glared. "It's nothing, okay?"

"Now you're getting defensive, which means it's actually something, and it's good." I chuckled. She growled; yet another cute thing she did.

"Fine, I'll stay in your room. Now, can you leave so I can get some rest?" I wondered if she showed anyone else that attitude. Then again, I doubted it, or else she'd be in someone else's room and they'd be fuckin' that attitude right outta her. Which wasn't a bad idea.

Shit, I wanted to watch her from under me as I slowly teased her with my cock and sunk slowly inside her pussy. I just knew she'd be wet and tight for me.

Fuck! I needed to get out of the room before my dick got its way and took what was mine.

Standing quickly, I went for the door. "I'll let you rest, sugar. You need some food first?" I didn't want her to sleep on an empty stomach, and Christ, I was glad I asked because her face softened and she gave me a small smile. My dick, once again, strained against its restraint.

"No, I'm fine. I had a big lunch with Ivy before my nap earlier. Thank you, though."

Opening the door, I said, "No worries. I'll be seeing you tomorrow. Night, babe."

"Night, Blue."

THANK FUCK the room next to mine was free; I didn't want to go far. I considered finding Talon, to see what he knew, but I was dead on my feet. I needed sleep, and just thinking I was sleeping next to Clary in some way had me giddy like a fuckin' girl.

Why did I have to lose my balls when feelings came into play? I swear Clary wore a new necklace with my hairy sack swinging around her neck.

The room was pretty much the same as mine. The bed was to the left of the room against the wall, the TV opposite it, hanging from some hooks on the wall. There were no large drawers like I had under my TV. Instead, there were only two little sets which sat on each side of the bed. At least there was a wardrobe to the right of the TV, and to the left was the bathroom.

All the rooms had their own bathroom. Talon did that as soon as he took over as president, and I was damned glad because I needed one. As I stripped off, I threw my gear to the floor and walked naked into the bathroom. I waited for the shower to heat up and thought how much I wished Clary was with me, wished she'd walk up behind me and gently wind her arms around my waist as she lay a kiss on my tattooed back.

Hell, my cock pulsated. I stepped under the spray of warm water and closed my eyes. All I could think about was Clary. I took my dick in hand and stroked as a groan fell from my lips. Clary's porcelain skin would be slick from the droplets of water as they ran down her small frame. I'd reach out to her and drag her closer so our bodies were aligned. One hand would go to her arse, while the other would thread through her hair, gripping tightly, and then I'd pull her head back so my mouth could attack her neck. She'd moan, and her pussy would be drenched from that one move.

Shit. I groaned as my cum shot out all over the tiled walls.

Dammit, I hadn't even gotten to the good part and she already had me coming apart.

I dried myself off with the towel I'd grabbed earlier from my room and slipped into some boxers. Finally, I crawled into bed. I couldn't help but chuckle to myself. Who'd have thought I'd come home to find myself already hooked to a woman. It was too soon, but fuck, I wouldn't have it any other way. She consumed my mind... even from that first sight of her sitting in that café.

And now she consumed my heart.

I'd do anything for that woman. Anything.

A SCREAM SLIPPED into my sleepy state and I bolted upright in bed. Where in the hell had that come from? Another scream and I jumped from the bed.

Clary.

I was out the door and in the hall when my eyes landed on someone walking into my room, where Clary was. Running, I dove onto his back and brought him to the floor. We both grunted and swore. Clary screamed again and thrashed around in the bed.

What the fuck?

The dude under me pushed back. I sat back and rolled him over. Billy stared up at me. "What the hell you doin', kid?" I asked. I stood and went to the side of the bed. Clary was sweating and whimpering.

Billy came up beside me and whispered, "I wasn't sneakin' in. I know she's yours, Blue. She's done this nearly every night she's been here. The nightmares."

"About what happened the other night?"

"Nah, I asked Wildcat to find out. I'm in the room opposite. I hear them break her every time. They're about the fire." He paused a second. "She eventually comes out of them herself. But on one night... fuck, don't kill me. One night, I climbed in next to her, and she seemed to settle."

"Out," I ordered. Goddammit, I hated that I wasn't there for her.

"Blue, I wasn't takin' advantage of her—"

I turned my head to him. "I know, kid." He was the youngest of our rowdy brotherhood, yet, sometimes he was the smartest. Though, the type of pussy he slept with wasn't all that bright. Still, we all went through that stage.

"'Kay," he uttered and left.

When the door closed behind him, I flipped back the covers and brought my woman, who was still whimpering, into my arms. She sighed deeply and settled straight away, and fuck, that made me want to take care of her that much more.

There was a bang out in the hallway. I was about to get back out of bed and kill the fucker if Clary woke, but then the words I heard next shocked the shit out of me, and I knew it wasn't any of my business.

A door opened. "Pick, you're drunk, man. Go to your own room."

"C'mon, Billy," Pick slurred.

"Just because I sucked your dick once doesn't mean I'm gonna do it again. Hell, especially when you're drunk. You'll wake up and freak like last time."

"Nah, I won't."

"No, Pick. Not happenin'. Go find a nice pussy to warm your dick."

"Jesus, there's only one pussy I want, and I can't have that. You know that, brother. You want her too, *and* my cock."

"This ain't happenin'."

Then a door slammed, and I heard Pick ask himself, "What the fuck is wrong with me?"

Holy shit. Yep, that was definitely none of my goddamn business.

CHAPTER ELEVEN

CLARINDA

I was certain Blue had come into my room last night. I could smell him more on the pillow next to me. But why would he have done that, and then not be there when I woke? That feeling of having him close continued for the next two weeks.

I asked him many times if he was in my room through the night. He either ignored my question or told me not to be silly. I knew it was happening; I wasn't going crazy. I even tried to stay awake many times. Never worked. I had his company only a few times during the day—six, to be exact. He told me he was busy with work and such. I felt let down, but then those times he'd touch me in a way which made my heart beat wildly or when he'd whisper in my ear that I looked nice, had me feeling hopeful.

Hope that something could start with us.

But then my emotions would do an about-face, and I'd be left feeling fucking annoyed.

The man pissed me off, as well. It could be put down to sexual tension, but it also had to do with him being bossy and possessive.

One time, when I was in the common room with Billy, Stoke, and Dodge, Blue came in and told me to get up and go to my room. I knew for a fact I was not wearing any see-through clothes. So I told him to get stuffed; he had no right to tell me what to do. His biker brothers laughed, and that was when I found myself over his shoulder and heard his brothers hoot and laugh.

He walked me into my room—I knew from the scent —set me on my feet, got close and whispered, "If I tell you to do something, you should."

"I think it's in your best interest, Blue," I hissed, "that you step back and apologise. You have no right telling me what to do, mister."

"I don't like the way they look at you."

"Pfft, I don't care. As far as I'm concerned, they can look however they want because none of them, or *anyone* for that matter, has asked me out, so I'm *free* to do what I want."

"Clary," he growled low and deep.

"Yes, Blue?"

"You're a pain in my arse."

"Fancy that, because you're a pain in mine also."

At a time like that, I wanted to see his face. Who was I kidding? I wanted to see it at all times. However, then especially, I wanted to be glaring in the right goddamn direction to get my point across. I was going to go bonkers if that man didn't take the next step and either ask me out or kiss me. Of course, I knew it was hard to go out on a real date. I wasn't even sure bikers did that, but the thought that my sister still wanted me, for whatever damn reason, was troubling. She hadn't even contacted me in any way.

I didn't know what was going on, and that frustrated me even more. I wanted things back to a semi-normal life. I mean, I knew it would never be the same. I could never trust her, and really, I never wanted to see her again, but I wanted my life back. I wanted to go to the library, to go to the supermarket—hell, I wanted to go out on the town with the new friends I had made.

However, I was still too scared to do any of that. Even though my girls had reassured me I'd be well protected, I didn't want to risk it until I knew my sister didn't still have a vendetta against me.

Whatever the fuck it was about.

The only thing which made me happy was that I had finally healed. My ribs no longer hurt, and as I felt my face while in the bathroom that morning, there were no signs of any tender spots. Moving out of the bathroom, I went to the bed and sat down then flopped back to lie down, only to sit straight back up when my door flew open.

"Enough of this staying at the compound all day and night shit," Deanna announced. "We're going to get our nails done and have crap put on our faces as a bonding time. It will be Hell, but I know you'll enjoy it. You seem like the girly-girl type."

"So am I," Julian giggled. His shadow stopped at my side and pulled me up by my elbow to stand. "Let's go, cherry pie. Zara's waiting in the car, and Ivy will meet us there."

"I'm not really in the mood, guys," I said.

"Stiff shit," Deanna stated. She took my other hand and guided me out the door.

"I had one of those this morning," Julian said.

"What?" Deanna asked as we walked down the hall. I knew there would be no point in arguing my point about staying; when Deanna and Julian wanted to do something for you, they got their way, whether you liked it or not.

"A stiff shit."

Deanna gagged. "Oh, my fucking God, gay man. T-M-motherfucking-I." I couldn't help but laugh at Deanna's reaction, because I knew Julian had only said it to annoy her, especially when he whispered in my ear, "I can get her every time."

The spa time was just what I needed. What also

helped was Deanna pestering me to spill why I was so uptight lately, besides the fact that my sister was a raging slut. The three of them had noticed my moods were fluctuating from day-to-day, hour-to-hour even. At first, as Julian had put it, they thought I was on my period, or due for it. However, I had never snapped out of it.

Sighing, I leaned back in the chair, where some lady was at the end pampering my feet. Julian sat on one side of me, while Zara sat on the other, and then Deanna was next to her.

"I don't know." I did, but I felt stupid for saying it. What should be foremost on my mind was my sister and her fucked-up-ness, but it wasn't. It was Blue.

"I call bull," Julian said. I was just about to tell him again that it was nothing when my phone announced I had a voice message.

I pressed play, and the automated voice said, "From Ivy Morrison at 1pm," followed by Ivy's excited, "Girl, oh, my God. I did it. I confronted Billy. He told me Blue comes into your room every night as soon as he knows you're asleep, because of your nightmares. Do you know what this means, woman?" She sang the next part, "He wants you; he likes you." The message ended, and I knew my face was red.

"I get it now," Zara said with a smile in her voice.

"Why didn't you tell us anything about what's been going on?" Julian asked in a small voice. He sounded upset, and I hated that.

"You're all close to him. I didn't want to make it awkward for you all, and Ivy's still kind of new to the group, like me."

"Honey," he started as he took my hand in his. "Us here, we have a code. It also includes Vi, Talon's sister, Ivy and you, and that code is for the sisterhood of bikers. Of course, I get to be a part of it, because I'm so awesome. But what that code means is anything you don't want to be passed on to the men, won't be. Shit, Pop-Tart, we talk about the men all the time. You've got to have this chance with the sister-hood to vent or else they would just drive you crazy. It's hard being around biker men. They drive differently than most men. They're... *more* than any other men in every way, and sometimes that can be too much to handle. Which is when you come to us. Now, we're glad you've gone to Ivy, but it's time to fill your other sisters in on what's going on."

Tears filled my eyes. Why hadn't I met these wonderful people so many years ago? I could have put up with anything if I had them at my side. Why couldn't any one of them have been my real sisters? I smiled to myself. Yes, even Julian... who still referred to me as his daughter around the bikers.

"Okay. I'll tell you everything."

"This is gonna be juicy," Deanna cackled and clapped her hands together.

"Not really. It's more frustrating than anything. Since Blue's been back, I haven't seen him much, but—before

Ivy said what she said in the message—I was sure he was coming to my room every night when I slept. I tried staying awake to catch him. I tried waking up early. However, I haven't had the chance to know for sure. Well, not until Ivy's message."

"That *would* be frustrating," Zara said.

I bit my bottom lip, contemplating if I should tell them the rest. Stuff it, they could help. They knew him better, and maybe what I had been reading in Blue, that he was interested in me, was wrong. "That's not all." My cheeks felt flushed, and I knew they were red. "I'm frustrated because he won't make a move on me. I know I shouldn't be caring about it right now, especially with everything going on, not that we know what's going on with my sister. But he's hot and cold all the time, and when he's hot—when he touches me, whispers in my ear —I want more. Then again, when he's a possessive freak when I'm around his biker brothers, it just annoys me. It's like he has this claim over me in front of them, but then he goes cold as soon as we're alone again."

"She's been around Ivy too much." Julian laughed.

"Damn straight," Deanna added.

"Guys," I whined.

"We get it now," Deanna continued. "You're sexually frustrated. I mean, I can understand that. Blue's hot. Not as hot as my man, but he's up there. What I don't get is why the guy's waiting. Shit, we've all seen the way he watches you. Griz has even said he needs to get his act together."

"Maybe…" Zara paused. "Maybe, he doesn't want to scare you off. Maybe he wants to take things slowly because you could be special to him. Talon and I were just talking about this last night. He's claimed you as his, honey, but—"

"What does that mean?" I asked.

"No other man can touch you without getting on Blue's bad side," Deanna said.

"Alpha men are so damn hot," Julian offered to the conversation.

"Then, if he's an alpha male and *has* claimed me, why isn't he… why doesn't he… why can't he—"

"Fuck you?" Deanna supplied.

I shrugged. "Um, I guess. Yes, that, but why won't he show me he does care? That he wants more from me?"

"Oh, he does, sugar plum. He has a boner every time he's around you. Believe me… I've noticed."

Wow. Really?

"He could be waiting to make a move for when all your shit's over," the new male voice made me jump. Julian screamed, and Deanna swore.

"Pick, what the fuck? You can't sneak up on us," Deanna snapped.

"Boss wants you to call him, Wildcat. You're not answering your phone. I caught Ivy out front. She's already headed back to the compound."

"Stuff it," Zara sighed.

Deanna teased her about something, but I wasn't interested in the conversation. I was busy thinking that Pick could be right. Maybe Blue thought he was doing the right thing by waiting until my problem was out of the way; however, I didn't want to wait.

It was about time I took matters into my own hands, even though I was so nervous. Still, there was a significant amount of frustration built up, and I was prepared to shove all my inexperience with sex out the window because I wanted my man.

"Hey, honey," Zara said with a sweet voice.

She must have had him on speaker because when I heard his voice, he sounded pissed. "What the fuck, Kitten? What. The. Fuck?"

"We had it under control," she replied.

"Give me the phone," we heard in the background, and I'd know that voice anywhere. Blue. Still, Talon said into the phone, "No." He must have been talking to Blue. "Zara, you better get your arse back here now. What in the hell were you thinkin', woman? You and your damn three *muff*kateer posse are in deep shit. Hopefully, Blue will cool down by the time you get back with his woman. I told you not to do this shit. I told you if she was to leave, she was to be guarded so Blue wouldn't lose. *His*. Shit."

He took an angry breath. "Guess what, Kitten? He lost his shit when he came into my fuckin' office to find out where his woman was, and I had to say I didn't know.

Thank fuck Billy saw your posse leaving with her. Then, I find out another brother saw *you*, Kitten, my damned woman, in a car out front, waiting to take Blue's woman out for a fuckin' joyride, telling no fuckin' one where you were going."

"Talon, honey." Zara sighed like she was used to him getting this mad. I couldn't understand how she was so calm; I was about to pee myself. "We needed a girl's day. We couldn't do that with any brother around."

"You needed a girl's day," he growled, and I was sure it was through clenched teeth.

"Yes," Zara stated. "It's not like we weren't covered. We've got our mace and Tasers."

Mace? Tasers?

"Well, damn, excuse fuckin' me. You had it all covered if someone grabbed the lot of you because you had your mace and Tasers." Okay, that was definitely sarcasm.

"Do not take that tone with me, Talon Marcus. You owed me for knocking me up anyway. My body went through hell for you."

Is she crazy?

"Kitten," he sighed.

What the hell? His voice took on a totally different tone. Had she just calmed his beast?

"Get your arse back here. And because you went through Hell for me, I'll try and stop Blue from killing you three stooges."

"That would be good, honey. See you soon."

I heard a click; the call had ended. I turned in my seat to face her way, and I uttered, "You are amazing."

She giggled. "Don't worry. You'll learn how to control them, too."

Pick scoffed behind us and barked, "Let's move."

I smiled to myself. It was time to step up and do what Zara had done: take charge. All I had to do was not chicken out before we got back.

A laugh bubbled up out of me. Finally, I felt I was getting my old self back.

CHAPTER TWELVE

CLARINDA

Julian helped me back into the compound with an arm around my shoulders. After we'd left the beautician's, the air had turned cold. I was grateful when we walked into the compound and the heaters were on, warming the place.

Because I had been there long enough, I knew Julian was leading me through the common area and down the hall opposite the one which held the bedrooms. We were heading toward Talon's office.

Zara and Deanna were in front of us, happily chatting as though they weren't about to walk into a room filled with pissed-off men. They must have opened the door to the office, because the next thing I heard was, "Never again, you hear me, Wildcat?" Blue growled low. "Never fuckin' again do you take her out without me or other brothers with you."

"Now, hang on—" Deanna started.

"Darlin', no," came Griz's gruff voice.

"You don't know what could happen. Until we sort this shit out, Clary's not to fuckin' leave without protection!" Blue yelled.

"We had—" Zara began.

"Kitten, no," Talon growled.

Zara sighed. I didn't like they were getting into trouble for doing something nice for me. Especially when I had such a good time.

I shrugged Julian's arm off and stepped forward. With my hands on my hips, I said, "Stop it, Blue. I'm fine; we're all fine, so you can stop beating your chest like some damned caveman. They did something nice for me because they could see I was down. So I will not have you yelling at them."

"Sugar—"

"No," I snapped. "And if I could see properly, I would storm out of this room so you'd know how annoyed you have made me, but I can't, so...." I turned toward Julian. "Please help me back to my room."

"Sure, buttercup."

"Don't you dare. I'll take her," Blue clipped.

I drew my lips between my teeth to hide the smile wanting to come forth. He had just played into my plan. I felt Julian's heat beside me, and he whispered, "Go get him, tiger." Oh, God, had I been that readable?

No matter. I was still going through with what I had planned. I think Blue also needed it. So as Blue came to my side and slid his arm around my waist, I nodded once to Julian.

No words passed between us as he walked me to my room. He was tense and still pissed; I could tell from the way his hand clenched on my top around my waist. I could also tell from his stiff posture.

He opened the door and manoeuvred me through. I walked off from his grip and over toward the bed, where I turned back to face him.

"Clary—" he began.

I spoke over him, "Do you find me attractive?"

The room fell silent while I waited with baited breath for his answer.

"Yes," he said simply.

"Good." I nodded, more to myself than anything. *This could work then.* "Would you kiss me?"

He groaned. "Sugar, you can't... you don't... dammit, you're making things hard."

I smiled. "Already? That was fast."

He choked on a startled laugh. "That's not what I meant. Fuck, woman, you're gorgeous, but now just isn't the right time."

Looking at the floor, I was disappointed. I was going

to have to play dirty. "So, you don't want me?" I was proud I sounded so deflated.

He was in front of me in seconds, his hand under my chin as he gently lifted my head upward. "I never said that. Christ, I want you in every way, but—"

Oh, no. He was *not* going to finish his thoughts. Instead, I felt for his face and held it between my hands, and then my lips were on his. It took seconds, only seconds before his shock wore off and he kissed me back. His head slanted to the side, and he deepened the kiss by biting my bottom lip, pulling it down, and then his tongue invaded my mouth. A moan fell from my lips. I wrapped my arms around his neck and went onto my tiptoes to get as close as I could to him. Still, I wanted more, and my body knew it. My panties already felt soaked from the thought of having Blue inside me.

Pulling away, I pressed my cheek against his so I could whisper in his ear, "I'd like very much to suck your cock, Blue."

"Fuck," he hissed. His hands clenched at my sides, just above my hips.

I kept my head where it was to hide the blush, and just in case he rejected me because I didn't want him to see my pained features.

He was still, his breath laboured, and then he breathed out as though it tormented him. "Clary…"

Please, no.

I was going to fight. I needed to fight for him. For us.

My hands slid down his arms, and before he realised what I was doing, they gripped his jeans at the top. I quickly managed to pop the top button and unzip his fly before he reacted. He grabbed my hands to still them, only he didn't remove them.

"We shouldn't—"

"Please," I begged.

Who was this woman? If I got the result I wanted, then I didn't mind the woman I had become right there in that bedroom.

"God, sugar. You make it so hard for me to be good. You deserve better, babe. You deserve time, courting. Fuck," he snapped and rested his forehead against mine. "I hate to say this right now, but it may get across the main message. I've had a heap of women, sugar, and I mean a lot." *Well, hell, that was a cold bucket of ice over me.* "But all of them have just been a place to slip my dick when I wanted to get off. None of them, and I fuckin' mean *none*, sugar, have made me want to get to know them. Have made me want to take my time with them. Have made me want to protect them."

Oh, that was *so* much better, like stepping into a warm bath. My hands were in his jeans, pulling his large penis out of its confinements. He was already hard, and I liked I'd done that to him. I managed one stroke in before his hand went over mine.

"Jesus, woman, you just don't give up. I want everything to be good for you. I want you to trust me before you let me take your body. Because once I'm in there, that's it. You. Are. Mine."

"Blue," I sighed.

"Yeah, sugar?"

"I love everything you just said—except about your past experiences—but honestly, you have driven me crazy for the last two weeks. I know you've been coming to my room each night to protect me from my dreams, but then in the morning, you're gone. You, Blue, in one of my darkest times in life, have shone through. You've shown me sweet and expect me not to be charmed by you. I am, Blue. I'm more than charmed. However, I'm frustrated, because I want you to kiss me. You're taking too long doing it your way. We need to try my way."

"And that would be?" I could hear the amusement in his voice.

"For you to let me do what I want to you."

"And here I thought I had all the right words, the right moves. But I'm getting outplayed by a little minx. Have at me, sugar. But be warned, you only have a minute before I take over and...*have*...you."

A tingle shot straight through to my groin. He chuckled, and I knew it was because he saw I was smiling widely.

Until, that was, there was a knock at the door.

Groaning in irritation, I flopped back on the bed behind me.

"What?" Blue barked.

I sat up. Blue's shadow was in front of me.

"Man, I just need to ask you something about a car we got in the workshop," came a voice I didn't know.

"Serious as fuck, Lumber. Not right now." I heard Blue shift and say to me in a low, sexy tone, "Now, where were we?" He ran a hand over my cheek, then bent and kissed me lightly on the lips. After he stood back up, my hands went to his hips and I felt something new at my lips. It was the tip of his cock. My tongue snaked out and licked the tip; it tasted salty. "Open wide, babe," he ordered, and just as I did, I felt him draw his hips back with my hands.

A knock on the door sounded again, and a voice called, "Blue, man?" which startled him. He jumped and misfired his thrust forward. Instead of his dick sliding into my mouth, it jabbed me in the eye.

"Shit, oh, hell. No, no, no. Oh… ow!" I yelled. Both hands covered my eye as it started to water and sting.

I felt Blue's hands trying to pry my hands away so he could check out the damage.

"No, just wait," I pleaded.

BLUE

"Fuck, sugar. Are you okay? Christ, baby," I asked. Of course, she wasn't okay, because—dammit all to hell—I just poked my woman in the eye with my dick. Later, I might be able to laugh about it with her, but right then she was in pain, and I had caused it... with my fucking dick. I'd been so turned on, so hard from the way she spoke, the way she took control of the situation, that I fucked it all up.

Suddenly, the door behind me flew open. In it stood Griz and Talon, Lumber just behind them.

"What the fuck?" I asked, and quickly tucked my dick back in my jeans. They both watched the movement, and then looked to Clary with a wary look on their faces.

"You tell us what the fuck. We came running when Lumber here told us he heard Clary screaming in the room."

"You'd think I'd hurt her?" I asked in outrage. I'd never lay a hand on a woman; they bloody knew that.

"Then why is she holding her eye?" Talon asked.

Looking at the floor, I hissed between clenched teeth, "Motherfucker."

"Blue," Talon said with a tone of warning. He'd want to know. Hell, so would Griz. We've all got a special hate for abuse.

"Lumber, get goin'," I said.

"But what about—"

"Now, man," I snapped, and he quickly disappeared.

"Guys, I'm really fine. Nothing happened," Clary said, trying to calm the fucked-up situation down.

"No offense, darlin', but we need to know from our

brother that everything is cool. He was the one to leave the office before all wound up, and then we come in here and see a sight I sure as fuck wished I'd never seen. Hell, Blue, I love you like a brother, of course, but seein' your cock don't do anything for me," Griz explained.

"No, really, please. Let's just drop it." She moved her hand away from her eye. "See? I'm fine."

Christ. It was all red and watery.

"Clary, we have to know—"

"No, you don't," she snapped. She was trying to protect me from humiliation.

"Babe," Talon sighed.

"I jabbed her in the eye with my dick," I spat out. Christ Almighty. I was a fucking biker, and yet I just damn well knew I had a blush on my cheeks.

Griz snorted through his laugh. Talon took a lungful of air down the wrong pipe and started coughing.

"Yeah, laugh it up, fuckers. But I swear if anyone finds out about this, I will kill you both," I growled. They were both still laughing their arses off. That was when I heard a small giggle behind me. I turned to Clary to find her with her hand over her mouth, trying to hide her laughter.

"Now you're laughing," I teased. At least the atmosphere had lightened, but I didn't want it at my expense, especially after what I'd just done. I'd fucking ripped the hot mood out and replaced it with amusement.

Damn.

I turned back to Griz and Talon, and ordered roughly, "You can both get the fuck out now, and close the bloody door after you." Without another word, because they were still fucking laughing, they left, shutting the door with a bang after them.

Still looking at the door, I felt a small hand on my thigh, and then it glided up to my waist as Clary stood and stepped toward me. For the first time, I wished she could see me, see what she did to me. I wanted the world for her. How could I possibly feel so strongly for someone I'd known for such a short time?

"Blue," she uttered.

"Yeah, sugar?"

She licked her lips. My eyes followed her tongue as it peeked out and ran over her sweet mouth, and then she smiled and said, "Please kiss me."

All humour fled the room. Sliding my fingers through her hair at the back of her head, I brought her flush against me and growled, "Gladly." Our lips touched tenderly at first. I didn't know what she was doing, but I was testing her out, seeing if she wanted to back out. But when her eyes fluttered closed, I pressed my lips against her again, harder. Her cute tongue sneaked out once again, and that time, my tongue was there to tangle with it. With my hand still in her hair, my grip tightened, and I pulled her head to the side to deepen the kiss. I felt her hands clutch my tee as she moaned around my mouth.

My cock was so fucking hard; it wanted in her wet spot, and if it didn't get there soon, it'd blow on its damned own just from having Clary's... *everything* surrounding me. Moving my other hand from her waist, I slapped it down on her arse and squeezed. She squealed, and in retaliation, she placed her hands on both of my arse cheeks and pinched hard. Of course, that caused my hips to involuntarily thrust forward, making my dick happy when it got to run up and down against her.

If we didn't slow this down, I was gonna fucking dry-hump her and come, embarrassing myself once more.

CHAPTER THIRTEEN

CLARINDA

*G*one was the shy, reserved woman, and in her place was a tigress knowing exactly what she wanted. I didn't know if it was because I had been taunted with touches and sweet words from the man before me; all I knew was I needed him inside me.

I felt empowered knowing what I wanted.

I felt… my normal self.

That was what I was like. I saw something—so to speak—that I liked, and took it.

Why now?

Why is Blue the cause of me coming out of my shell?

Maybe it was because he'd shown me I mattered.

I broke the kiss, panting hard, and pried my hands

from Blue's delicious butt. I took hold of his tee and pulled it over his head. Thankfully, he didn't fight me on it. I then ran my hands over the planes and dips of his chest and stomach, enjoying every groove and bump, even counting his six-pack.

"I think someone else needs their top off," Blue growled, his hot breath fanning over my face. With a smile upon my mouth, I placed my arms directly in the air. He chuckled, raised my tee over my head and threw it. His hands were back on my sensitive skin straight away. He ran his hardworking hands over my hips, my stomach, my back and then, finally, he cupped both breasts, one in each hand. A soft sigh fell from my lips. His hands warmed my chest through my bra, but I wanted to feel his skin on mine. Reaching around my back, I unhooked my bra and drew it from my body. His hands left me for all of a second, and it was funny how I missed his touch. A shudder rippled through my body as his hands went back to my bare breasts. My head fell back and I moaned softly. Blue, not one to miss an opportunity, attacked my neck with his lips, tongue and teeth, while I ran my hands appreciatively over his back, encouraging him to keep going.

"Yo, Blue," someone called from the other side of the door.

Blue growled deep against my neck and lifted his head to yell, "Whoever the fuck it is had better disappear before I get my gun out."

We both heard feet quickly retreating from the door.

"You have a gun?" I asked. I mean, I knew he was a biker, and bikers were bad-arses, but I didn't know he carried a gun. I never thought of it actually. Did all of them carry guns while I was walking freely around the compound? Did horrible things happen all the time to warrant all bikers to carry guns?

"Sugar," he said in a way which sounded like I was being stupid for even asking.

"Do you always carry a gun?" I asked.

"Baby, I really don't want to talk about this while I have you half-naked in my arms."

"Blue, sweetheart, if you want to keep me half-naked, or even try and get me all-naked, then we are talking about this."

He muttered something under his breath and then sighed deeply. "Clary, I'm a biker. Sometimes we need protection and to be safe always, 'cause you never know when a situation could arise. It's best to be prepared and carry a weapon."

I pondered on that for a moment, and then asked, "What type of situation?" I was being stupid; I knew I was, and I didn't know why. I wanted the man—that, I knew for sure—but was I really ready to be involved with someone who carried a damned gun everywhere, in case a 'bad situation' arose? Thoughts of Zara, Deanna and Ivy ran through my head. They knew the situations; they were the cause of some of them. These bikers did things to protect their people. Could I look past everything and just lay my life on that belief for this man?

I believed I could.

"Situations like this; I'd about kill anyone who interrupted us right now."

I rolled my eyes. "Do you often get in situations like this with other women and threaten your biker brothers' lives?"

"Now that's not...no, well, uh...maybe I should just stop explaining things."

"Yeah." I glared. "Maybe you should just shut up."

"Maybe you should shut me up," he offered with a smile in his voice.

"Gladly." Feeling my way up his arms, I wrapped them around his neck and brought his mouth down to mine. We kissed hungrily and I loved it. I reached for his jeans and undid the button, and as I slowly slid down the zipper, Blue's hand came down on mine.

He pulled away from our kiss and with a heavy breath, he asked, "Fuck, Clary, are you sure?" I didn't answer. I couldn't; I was too focused on his hand as it travelled down between my legs, where he roughly rubbed me through my jeans. "Because, like I said, once I'm in here, it's mine. You're mine. Do you understand that?"

Nodding, I closed my eyes and whispered, "Yes."

"Christ, okay," he hissed. I didn't get to reach into his jeans for my prize, because he picked me up and gently laid me on the bed. His heat left me as he stood, his shadowy form just above me. It came closer as I felt his hands on my jeans. He undid the button and zipper then with eager motions, he pulled them and my panties from my body. He hissed once again, and groaned, "Fuck, you're gorgeous."

He trailed his hands up my legs slowly, and as he did, he parted them. I heard him kneel to the floor, his shoulders knocking my legs wider. "I'm gonna taste your sweet pussy, sugar. I've jerked off to just the thought of your taste," he admitted, and boy, did I love the thought of him touching himself while thinking of me. I jumped slightly when I felt his fingers spread my lower lips, and at the first touch of his tongue on my clit, I moaned. That was when he showed his control was slipping. He sucked, licked and tongued my clit and entrance with wild movements, driving me crazy the whole time, and a sudden orgasm was pulled from me as soon as he placed his finger inside me. My pussy clamped down around it and continued to pulse until it passed.

"I-um...wow." I licked my lips, my cheeks heating. "Uh, sorry...it's been a while," I said.

"I'll never fucking get tired of watching you lose control and come hard. Damn beautiful sight." He gave me one last lick and stood. I heard his pants fall to the floor. He must have quickly kicked them aside, because next he was ordering me, "Move up a bit, baby."

I shifted up on the bed so I was more or less in the

centre. Blinking through what light we had in the room, I saw and felt him move beside me. A drawer was opened when I heard the plastic tear. I knew he had slipped a condom on. In the next moment, the tip of his cock was at my entrance. That was until I held up my hand and it hit his chest as I said, "Wait."

"What's wrong?" he asked. "Am I moving too fast?"

Smiling, because I thought it was sweet he was worried, I told him, "No, I would... if you want, um... I would like to...." Stuff it. Why was it so hard for me to say what I wanted to do to him? Yes, it had definitely been a very long time since I'd been around a male, and honestly, I'd never been around one like Blue. I felt like a flustered teenager again, shy about everything. He was a man's man, a man who I wanted to please, and I was worried I wouldn't. Still, I sucked it up and said once again, "I really do want to suck your cock."

He moaned, "Damn, Sugar, those words from your sweet mouth are fuckin' hot, but I'm not sure I could last if I had my cock in your gorgeous mouth."

Pouting, I said, "I'd like to try." He groaned and I stopped the giggle wanting to escape, because I knew I was going to get my way. The bed dipped as he moved up toward my head. I heard a snap beside my head; he was removing the condom and then his form arched over me. His hands moved to the other side of my head as he lined his cock up with my lips.

"You won't always get your way, woman. Just this

once," he said, and then he moved forward; the tip of his cock touched my lips and I licked it. Opening wide, I reached up and gripped his thighs, pulling him closer to me as he slipped his large cock deeper into my mouth. He moaned low and pulled back out, only to push it back in. Soon, he was fucking my mouth with swift motions, and it was so bloody glorious. The feel of his cock sliding in and out of my wet, eager mouth was a real turn-on. My hands on his thighs tightened, encouraging him to continue his assault on my mouth.

"Fuck, fuck... I have to stop," he groaned and slipped all the way out. I must have complained with a whimper, because the next thing he said was, "When we have all the time in the world, and it's not our first, we'll do that all fuckin' night long, sugar. But I want in your pussy to claim it, and that's happenin' right now." He shifted on the bed, and again, he was between my legs. Roughly, eagerly, he moved them farther apart. "You want this, yes?" he asked, his voice strained.

"A million times, yes... please," I sighed.

"Fuck, you're tight," he clipped as he pushed a finger inside me, only to remove it and run it up my slick pussy lips. "And you're so wet for me, sugar. I fuckin' love that."

"Blue, if you don't get a move on, we'll get interrupted, and then *I'll* have to kill someone."

A laugh left his mouth. I felt the bed shift and him lean to the right as a drawer slid open, and there was a tear of a wrapper again. Soon enough, he lined himself up and slowly pushed inside my tight entrance. That was when all humour left him and he groaned as I moaned with pure pleasure. He filled me to the maximum. He was so big I swear I felt him hitting my cervix on the first go.

"Ah, hell, it feels so good, sugar; so fuckin' good. Christ, so, so fucking tight." He thrust deeper, causing a gasp to fall from my lips.

"Blue, oh God. You feel good inside me." I pulled him down on top of me so I could ravish his mouth. He gave back as good as I was giving.

Not sure if it was the moment, but I was sure we were made for each other.

"Oh, oh, I'm going to come," I moaned as another climax shuddered through my body, my pussy walls clenching around him.

He groaned. "Hell, fuck yes. Baby, yes. Milk me. I'm gonna come." He kept plunging inside me over and over. A grunt left his lips and then he groaned, and I felt his cock pulse inside me as he filled the condom.

All of his weight hit my smaller frame and I wrapped him in my arms, totally satisfied. I never wanted him to leave. I never wanted the moment to end and have reality rip its way through…but that could never happen.

Tears brimmed my eyes. I wanted my shit dealt with so I could continue on with a normal life. I wanted Blue to know me, not from protecting me, not from what I had to deal with, but just me, as I was in the compound with him. I wanted all that out in the real world. But first, I had to figure out what my sister really wanted.

He picked himself up, and he must have looked down at the tears leaking from my eyes, because he said, "Shit, sugar. Did I hurt you?"

"No, never. You could never hurt me. It's just…it was a lot to feel." I grinned shyly up at him.

"It was," he said with a smile in his voice. He got to his hands and I felt him leave my body, his cock sliding from within me, and all I wanted to do was drag him back down.

I was feeling too much.

"Sugar, please fucking tell me you're on the pill?"

"Yes," I uttered. I had to be, to ease the pain I received every month during my period.

"I'm clean, baby, and next time I wanna slide inside you bare, so I can feel all of you surrounding me. You good with that?"

"Um… yes, very much so." I licked my lips. "Blue, I, ah, I want you to know I'm clean, too. I've only ever had one man before you."

"Christ, sugar. In one way, I wanna cover my ears and sing la-la-la so I can pretend I never heard my woman had another. Then again, I'm so fuckin' grateful to know that you haven't had many. I'm the last one, though," he stated and climbed off the bed.

"You're… not leaving?" I asked, a weak tremor in my voice. I felt pathetic.

"No way, baby. I'll just get rid of this and then I'm coming back here... always." He kissed me tenderly on my lips, and then his footsteps were walking toward the adjoining bathroom.

I was left with my thoughts for a second, and it was enough time to know I had to do something, and soon, especially if I wanted to see where everything was going with Blue. I had to get rid of my trouble. It was time to form a plan.

CHAPTER FOURTEEN

ONE WEEK LATER

CLARINDA

*I*t took me a while to figure out what I was going to do. I knew I wouldn't be able to do it on my own, so I went for some help and hoped they would be willing. I was sure they were as sick of babysitting me as I was sick of staying at the compound twenty-four-seven, even though Blue had kept me thoroughly entertained. However, some of those times I was sure it was an excuse to keep me away from Zara, Deanna, Julian, and Ivy when they called in for a visit. Maybe he knew I was forming a plan to get out of my trouble.

Either way, it had to stop so I could breathe easy; not only me, but everyone around me.

I knocked on Talon's office door. Blue was out in the mechanical area for some reason, and I needed to use the time alone to get things started.

"In," Talon snapped on the other side of the door. I felt for the handle and turned it, slowly pushing it open, and stepped in. The room was bright, so I could easily see the hazy form of Talon sitting behind a desk to the right of the room. "Clarinda, what's up?" Shock showed in his voice.

Walking in further, I guided my way over to the front of his desk in hopes there was a chair to sit in. When I found one, I felt around and planted my bottom in it safely. I sat straight in a confident pose, even though I was rattled on the inside. Both Talon and Griz scared me a little, and even though I heard enough from Zara and Deanna that they were both softies on the inside, I still felt intimidated by them.

"I-I would like to talk to you about something, if you have time."

His chair creaked; he was leaning back in it. "I have time. What did you need to talk about?"

Licking my dry lips, I said, "I have a plan, and I need some help to… follow through with it."

"Why have you come to me and not your old man?"

I bit my bottom lip. I did feel terrible for not talking to Blue about it. However, I knew he would say no, and I

BLACK OUT

needed to do it. I lifted my head and told him the truth. "I know he wouldn't like my plan because it involves risking me."

"What makes you think I'll fuckin' like it then?"

"Because I'm sure you're as tired as I am with how things are progressing. We need to do something to get answers. I'm sick of staying at the compound all the time. I want a life back out there. I want to feel safe going places with Blue and the girls. We have nothing to go on—"

"That's not true."

"What do you mean?" I demanded.

"What has Blue told you?"

Shaking my head, I sighed. "Nothing."

"Maybe he thinks that's for the best."

"How can it be? It involves me. I should know everything," I snapped.

"True."

"Can you tell me?" I questioned carefully.

He chuckled. "Blue has given me shit in the past, so I don't see why not. We found out your sister wanted to keep you around for the money you'll come into when you hit twenty-five."

Closing my eyes, I dipped my head. Money. It was all about money. Not just the amount she was getting from being my caregiver, but she wanted my inheritance, as well. Question was, how would she have gone about getting it?

"Do you think…." I asked the floor. "Do you think she would have killed her own sister for that money?"

"No." His quick answer shocked me.

"Why?"

"She's a shit fuckin' sister, but she would never have wanted you dead. She's mixed up in drugs and with the wrong people. How she would have gotten your money, we don't know."

"How did you find this out?"

"We have a brother hangin' with those wrong people. They talk."

"Is there anything else?"

"They're watching, waiting to nab you, which is why Blue is so protective."

"Right," I snorted. "So really, there's no way I can have a life if this isn't…completed."

"What are you gettin' at woman?"

"Send me out there, on my own. Let them take me and you can follow, find out what their plan is, and then stop them."

Silence filled the room.

I jumped when a voice said behind me, "I don't like it, brother." I spun in my seat to see an outline of a body in the corner, sitting on what must be a couch. I'd never mistake the deep grumble. I just wish I'd searched the room before heading straight in. At least then I would have seen Griz… in a way.

"It may be our only option," Talon said.

"Blue won't go for it."

"He doesn't have to know," I offered.

"Darlin'—" Griz started.

"No. I want to do this, and yes, I know Blue won't let it happen, but come on. How long do I have to live like this? Until you have all your answers about what's happening? I—"

"That sounds like a fuckin' better idea than offerin' your own goddamn head on the line," Griz barked.

"I don't want to wait. It's driving me insane, and it's my own bloody head to offer!" I snapped and withdrew a deep breath. "Besides," I added softly. "You'll all be there to help."

"Talon," Griz pleaded.

He scoffed. "She'll have protection the whole time. Not only from us, but we'll get Vi and her crowd in, too."

"Fuck," Griz bit out through clenched teeth. He shook his head. "He'll kill you for doing this."

"I guess I can call it payback for all the shit he caused with Zara." Talon laughed. "There's also the fact that Clary would stop him. Ain't that right, babe?"

"Of course. I'll be indebted to you if you help me, and in return, I won't let Blue kill you. He'll be in enough shit from me for not telling me the information he had to bother about anything else."

Griz scoffed. "That I doubt, lady." He sighed. "You know I'll have your back, brother. You lead like always, but I don't fuckin' agree with it. Let that be noted. If it was the other way around, if it was Wildcat, you'd fuckin' kill anyone who helped her."

Talon chuckled. "I'd try, yeah. At least Clary came to us instead of our wild bunch of women, doing this behind all of our backs. She'll be safer that way, and he'll know it and realise it, after some time."

"Yeah, we'll fuckin' see."

With a smile in his voice, Talon asked, "So what's your plan, babe?"

My PLAN HAD BEEN SIMPLE. While Blue was distracted, I was to escape, walk right out of the compound and into a waiting taxi, where it would take me to the library. On a day Deanna wasn't working, of course. I didn't and could never want to risk the ladies' lives, even though they would all be up for it.

However, two days later, when I was in that taxi on my way alone, I was scared out of my mind.

Following me were Vi, Talon's sister, along with Warden and Butch, all of whom I'd met the day before. There was also Talon, Pick, Dodge, and Billy in another vehicle following them. Stoke was already planted at the library, ready to watch me when I arrived. Griz had opted to stay back at the compound and be there for when Blue found out and went crazy. I doubted he would, but then Griz laughed and said to never doubt a man and his emotions when it came to his woman.

The taxi stopped, and I handed over some money I had in my hand. I wasn't sure if I was over-tipping or not, and I had actually forgotten about payment until Talon shoved money in my hand as I was leaving.

Climbing out of the car, I blocked my eyes from the sudden assault of bright light. The sun was really warm, adding to the worried sweat on my back and hands. I was used to walking into the library, so I knew my way without getting into trouble. Once inside the cool, air-conditioned room, I made my way to my usual desk. Already there for me would be Stoke, as we'd planned, and also on the table would be an audio novel, to keep up the pretence I was there to read and be alone, not there for an ulterior motive.

My hands slid over the table and landed on the audio book. I was to place the headphones on my ears and listen to it, only in a low tone, so I could still hear what was going on around me. Turning it on, the lady's voice started and announced I would be listening to *Fifty Shades of Grey*. My head came up to the darker form across from me, Stoke. That was when I heard a deep, manly chuckle.

I'd heard many stories about the book, like it was Viagra for women. However, I had never intended to read it. Bloody Stoke. I was soon learning he was the practical joker amongst the biker brothers.

It was an hour later, when Anna had been saved by Christian Grey, Stoke's phone rang. I moved my headphones away so I wouldn't be distracted, because I was now really hooked on the storyline and wanted to see where it led.

"Talk," he answered. "Shit, yes, yes. Okay, we're out." He stood quickly; I heard his chair being scraped back on the carpet. "Sweetheart, we need to go." He came around the table and gripped my elbow, helping me out of the seat.

Once we were walking, I asked, "What's going on?"

"They followed you, but aren't making a move. The boss is gonna try and nab one of them for interrogation. We need fuckin' answers."

"Okay, all right." I nodded.

Stoke's hand moved to my waist and he said, "Climb in, darlin', and we'll head off." He helped me into a car. I listened and waited for him to climb in the other side. That was when I heard a sound on the outside of the car, and suddenly, the driver's door was flung open.

"You stupid idiot," my sister's voice roared. "Everything would have been perfect if you just went along with it and not fucking involved the bikers."

"Amy? Amy, where's Stoke?"

"Getting the shit beat out of him." The car started and I grabbed her arm.

"No, no, you're not taking me!" I screamed.

"You don't get it, *sister*," she sneered. "If I don't, they'll kill you. I never wanted you dead, never. Just like our parents. I couldn't stop them from killing them, but I can stop them from killing you."

"Amy," I gasped. "Y-you, they… oh my God. No, Amy."

"Shut up and let go."

"No. This was all about fucking money? I would have given it to you if it meant your friends would leave me alone."

She shoved me hard to the side, my head banging against the window as the car took off onto the road. "Fuck this whole thing!" she screamed and took a big gulp of breath. "I never wanted it to be like this. I just wanted to scare you. I was going to sell you, you stupid bitch, to some rich guy, and you would have lived the life. But now, he doesn't want anything to do with it, because you got the fucking bikers in it. You ruined everything."

Sitting up, I scoffed. "So damn sorry I ruined your goddamn plan to sell me, your own fucking sister!" I yelled. "What now, Amy? What are you going to do now?" I asked as I felt for my seat belt; she was driving like a mad woman and I wanted to be safe. I snorted to myself —if I could be safe.

"We need to get out of here. I won't let them kill you, but you will be giving me your money when you turn twenty-five, and *then* I'll leave you the hell alone."

"Why do any of this, Amy? You caused our parents' death. How can you live with yourself?"

"I had no choice. I was in a hard place and needed

money. You wouldn't get it. You're too fuckin' perfect. Fuck!" she shouted and slammed on the brakes. My hands blindly reached out in front of me, hitting the dash. "Shut the fuck up!" she screamed at me. "I nearly went through a red light." She laughed maniacally. "Then we'd both be dead."

"Amy, please don't do this. Please, take me back. They can help you, and then I'll give you the money. I promise."

She snorted. "Yeah, I've been watching, Rinda. You just want to go back to that hot biker of yours. Not happening, sister. We do this my way."

Glass smashed. I screamed and covered my head. Amy swore and yelled, but one voice overtook all sounds.

"Get the fuck out now," Blue growled. "Clary, are you okay?"

"Y-yes," I stuttered through my shock. How did he find me?

"Fucking shit!" Amy screeched. Movement around me had me thinking Amy was getting out of the car, or she was being dragged out.

My door opened. My hands went to my chest in fright. "Come on, babe. Let's get out of here before we get more attention," a different voice came.

"Don't fuckin' start with me, Talon," Blue snarled.

"You didn't have to smash the window out, brother. The goddamn doors were unlocked."

"No, they weren't," I said quietly. I remembered my

elbow hitting the door lock on the window when we braked.

"Come on, guys," Stoke called from somewhere. I sighed in relief, glad to know he was okay. No sooner had Talon helped me out, someone got in and the car took off.

Two figures, one struggling, came toward Talon and me. "Swap," Blue hissed. Talon released my arm and I was lifted into two strong ones. Blue's scent invaded my senses, calming me. Even though I knew he was furious, I was glad he was before me and I was in his arms.

CHAPTER FIFTEEN

AN HOUR EARLIER

BLUE

*W*alking back from the mechanic's shop at the compound, I was pissed once again. In the past week, I'd kept getting called away from Clarinda for stupid fuck-ups which any of the other main guys could have fixed. I knew my woman was getting sick of being cooped up all the time, so I wanted to stick by her, entertain her in a way. I grinned; some entertainment was more fun than others. Just that morning, I woke up my woman with my dick buried inside her.

When I had woken before her, she was sound asleep beside me. She was extra tired from waking yet a-fuckin'-gain from her nightmares. I would do anything to take them from her.

I *was* going to let her sleep and just get up to go check a few things out, but then she stretched and made a purring sound. There was no way in Hell I could resist that.

So, as she slept, I was able to flip the blankets away, gently spread her legs and climb between them. She'd gone to sleep naked from our nightly romp, and I was damn glad.

She came to life. Her eyes opened, she smiled and then moaned as my dick and mouth took her hard and fast at the same time, desire running throughout her body. Even though she couldn't see me, she knew it was her biker doing his duty to please his woman. It didn't take her long to reach her climax, and when she did, she came hard, her juices squirting out and onto the sheets.

Fucking glorious.

Just thinking of it had me hard, and I was eager to get back to her. I wanted to see how much I could get her to squirt again. I'd never had a woman who could do that, so I was more than ready to play.

The compound was quiet, and straight away, I knew something was going down. I bolted to our room, only to find it barren. So I went to the kitchen; no one was there.

I went to the dining room, but again, empty. I walked down the other hall to the farthest room to see if Talon was in his office and if he knew where my woman was. I was fuckin' worried the other women had taken her for another joyride.

When I opened the door, my eyes landed on Griz sitting behind the desk. He looked grim and serious all in one, and suddenly, my heart plummeted to my balls and I swear to Christ they both whimpered.

"Where. Is. She?" I demanded through clenched teeth. My hand tightened on the handle of the door; it was either that or I'd be smashing through shit.

"She came to Talon a couple of days ago with a plan. They're out now doin' what she wanted, to get her life back to where she wants it, for you and her."

"Fuck!" I roared, stepping into the room and planting my fist through a wall. "Talon allowed this? He took my woman from safety and allowed this fuckin' shit?"

"I s'pose you could say your woman talked him into it."

"Where are they?"

"Just let this shit happen, brother. Talon has her covered at all times."

"Where in the fuck are they, *brother?*"

"It's goin' down at the library."

"Right," was my parting word before I ran out to my Harley, with Griz following me while on his phone. No doubt, he was warning Talon I was comin'.

So fucking be it.

Talon was about to get ripped a new arsehole.

We arrived at the library as Talon was getting in a black SUV. I stalked up to the side of it, grabbed his tee and dragged him out of it. Dodge was in the driver's seat with a surprised look on his face.

I shoved him against the car and got in his face. "Where is she? She better be safe or I'll fuckin' kill you."

"Her sister just hijacked her in Stoke's car. Get the fuck in before we lose them."

"Fuck, fuck, fuck," I chanted as I let him go and climbed in the passenger's side. Talon climbed in the back and Griz followed on his Harley. I left mine at the curb of the library, and for once in my damned life, I didn't give a shit if it was stolen. I just needed to get my woman back and safe.

Dodge took off, burning down the road. It didn't take us long to catch the car, and when they braked heavily at a red light, I jumped out and ran to the vehicle, which was four cars in front of us. I took one look and saw Clary in the passenger side looking freaked the fuck out. There were no other thoughts which passed but to get her out, so I smashed in the driver's side window, unlocked the door and dragged her screaming bitch sister out.

"Get the fuck out now," I growled and then asked, "Clary, are you okay?"

"Y-yes," she stuttered.

"Fucking shit!" my woman's sister screeched.

Talon was at Clary's side getting her out of the car. "Come on, babe. Let's get out of here before we get more attention," he said to her.

"Don't fuckin' start with me, Talon," I snarled.

"You didn't have to smash the window out, brother. The goddamn doors were unlocked."

"No, they weren't," Clary whispered.

"Come on, guys," Dodge called. Butch showed up out of nowhere, got in the driver's seat, and took off before the cops showed. We hoped no one had enough time to take down plate numbers.

With a struggling bitch, I walked to Talon, who had a hand on my woman, and with a fierce glare, I hissed, "Swap."

As soon as I had Clary, I picked up her small, shaking body in my arms and carried her to the car which Dodge was still in, idling away. I was majorly pissed still, but I was so fuckin' happy to have her in my arms. I climbed in the back and placed her in my lap; there was no way I was letting go.

I wasn't sure what Dodge was waiting for, but I wanted to get the fuck out of there, get my woman back to our room and give her a good and goddamn proper spanking.

The passenger door next to Dodge opened, and in jumped Talon.

"Where's that motherfuckin' bitch?" I asked.

"In the car with Vi and Warden."

"D-did..." Clary cleared her throat. "Did you end up getting one of the men?"

Talon turned in the seat and looked at her. She must have felt his gaze, because she turned her head from my chest and looked his way.

"No, babe. We nearly had him, but then we got a call about what was goin' down with you and Stoke."

"Is Stoke okay?"

"I'm fine, sweetheart, and thanks for carin'." Clary jumped when Stoke called out from the back of the car. What in the fuck was he doing in the trunk?

"We just need to get him to the hospital to get checked out," Talon said.

"That doesn't sound okay to me," Clary said sadly.

"Sweetheart, I've had worse. My ribs are hurting; that's all, which is why I'm lying in the back here."

"You're in the trunk?" Clary cried out. She wiggled around on my lap, causing my dick to harden at the wrong time.

Christ, I was mad as hell, and yet the woman could get my body worked up.

"Stop, stop the car!" she yelled. "He can lay in here on the seat. Blue and I will go in the trunk."

"Clary," Talon started. She turned in his direction. "It's damn nice for you to be concerned about a brother, but we're nearly there anyway. Calm down. We'll get Stoke looked at, and then we'll deal with your sister."

She nodded and relaxed back into me. "Blue," she whispered.

"Hmm," I replied.

"Don't be too angry with your friends. I put them up to it all."

"We'll talk about it later," I said.

She stiffened. "Blue—"

"I said we'll talk about it later," I growled over her.

She let out an annoyed sigh and added, "Fine. We will do that, and you can also tell me why you've kept things from me."

Through clenched teeth, I bit out, "I s'pose Talon was the one to inform you of said shit?"

"I… uh, well—"

My arms tightened around her.

"No fuckin' need to say, Clary. I know, and he'll get what's comin' to him. Won't you, *brother*?" I growled, knowing he was listening in.

"Lookin' forward to it," was Talon's reply.

WE DROPPED Stoke and Dodge off at the hospital, and Talon drove us straight to Vi's PI office, where they'd be keeping Amy in a holding cell. I climbed out of the SUV first, onto the busy street, and then gripped Clary's hips to help her down. Griz soon pulled up behind us on his Harley, and as soon as he was off, I said, "Griz, take Clary. I want a word with Talon."

"Fuck," he uttered. "Sure, Blue." He wound a hand around Clary's upper arm and pulled her off toward the office.

That was, until Clary wouldn't move with him. "No," she demanded. "Blue Skies, you do not need to have 'a word'," she used her hands for quote marks—hell, she was cute—"with Talon. It was my choice to do this. I knew you wouldn't help. I knew you'd hate the idea, because you like to wrap me up in bloody cotton wool so nothing touches me. But I'm sick of it, Blue. So sick of it. I love where we stay, and I love the people there, but it isn't a home. It's not normal to stay within so many walls all the damned time."

"She's right, brother. You wouldn't have listened to her," Talon said, and that was when I saw red.

I approached him and got in his face to yell, "And you thought you had the fuckin' right to listen to her? To do what she said, when it caused her to be in fuckin' danger?"

"Jesus, she was never really in danger, Blue. You'd know that if you calmed the fuck down," he snapped back, which was when I shoved him.

"Blue, do not do anything to Talon."

"What gives you the damn right? She is *my* woman, Talon. *Mine*."

Talon rolled his eyes. "Shit, brother, I know she's yours; you piss on her every time another male is near her. Hell, I wanted things back to normal, too. I wanted her safe and free so you can *both* breathe easy."

"Fuck, Talon. Fuck!" *Motherfucking shit.* I knew he was right. I knew he had my woman's back, but it'd never change the fact he went behind my back and put her in danger.

Talon chuckled. "Call it payback for what you did to Zara."

"What the fuck?" I bellowed and punched my brother and best friend in the face. He stumbled back but stayed on his feet.

Hearing the smack-down, Clary screamed, "Blue, stop!"

But I couldn't. I was livid. "Payback? How in the fuck is that payback? I only cottoned on to Zara, told her I was interested if you two didn't go far. How in the fuck is puttin' my woman in a bad situation goddamn payback?" I yelled.

"You wanted Zara?" I heard a soft voice say behind me.

Christ.

I turned to my woman. "That was ages ago, sugar, and I knew then I didn't have a chance. She only had eyes for this fucker." I thumbed behind me to Talon, not that she'd see it.

"Are you still hung-up on her? Do you still have feelings for her?" she questioned.

I walked to her, and Griz let go and backed up a step. My hands went to her cheeks and I brought her face up so I could study it. "No," I stated. "That ended a long fuckin' time ago. I do not feel anything for her."

Watching her, I could see her thinking something over, and then the cunning little wench said, "I'll believe you, and I'll drop this whole eye-opening conversation, if you stop this manly-beating-each-other-up-but-you-still-love-him shit."

I was stunned stupid. I froze, my mouth wide, my eyes wider. Talon laughed behind me as Griz guffawed behind her.

"Damn, man. You're gonna need all the luck with that one," Talon said, still chuckling as he patted me on the back.

Clary stood tall and asked, "Do we have a deal? Oh, and I'll also forgive you for forgetting to tell me some important things, like why my sister was really gunning for me."

Over Clary's shoulder, I saw Griz turn so his back was to me and bend over, pissing himself laughing.

Shaking my head, I said, "You, Miss Clarinda James, are a piece of work. You do realise you're bribing your old man?"

She smiled wide. "Yes. Now, do you accept, so we can go in and talk to my sister?"

"Fuck me," I uttered. I pulled her close and touched my lips to hers, saying against them, "Talon's damn lucky you are unharmed, and *you're* damn lucky you're so fuckin' sweet. Yes, I accept." And then I kissed her. She wrapped her arms around my shoulders and I wound mine around her waist, dragging her closer so we were hip-to-hip.

Being so wrapped up in my woman, knowing she was safe, we didn't hear the car pull up out front of Vi's, and we didn't hear Wildcat, Hell Mouth, Julian, Ivy, and Killer climbing out of it. So, I also didn't know Talon had put his hand up to keep them quiet as they approached.

She pulled away first, and I growled low to show I wasn't happy. She grinned at me and reached up with one hand to cup my cheek. "We need this sorted." She felt my nod and removed her hand so she could rest her head against my chest, where she said, in such a sad tone it hurt my ears to hear, "My sister admitted to me it was her so-called friends who killed our parents. She had her part in it, Blue. How could a person do that? It was all over... all for money?"

"Christ, sugar. I don't know. That's something no one can understand."

"She said she was going to sell me. She didn't want me dead like her friends did. She was going to *sell her own sister*, Blue." I felt her hand wrap around in my tee. I was outraged a sister would even think of doing such a thing. I was outraged it was my woman going through the emotions which had suddenly hit her as the situation calmed a bit.

"It'll never happen," I whispered into her hair, my glare on the footpath.

"It won't. He doesn't want me, now that you're all involved, b-b-but..." her breath hitched. "They still want me dead because of the money I'll have when I turn twenty-five. They want me dead so my sister will get everything."

A door slammed. We both pulled our heads up in the direction of Vi's office door being banged closed and we caught sight of the back of Deanna's body entering the building. I looked over Clary's head to see two teary women, Wildcat and Ivy.

"Sugar, I just have to do something." *Before Hell Mouth kills your sister.* "Stay here with Ivy and Zara. I'll be back real soon, yeah?"

She sniffed and nodded. "Zara and Ivy are here?"

Ivy moved up to one side of Clary, and Zara on her other side, but it was Ivy who said, "We're here, sweetie. Come on; there's a bakery just down the road. We'll let our guys do some stuff, and then they can come get us."

Killer stepped up to the women and said, "I'll go with them."

Sending a chin lift to him, I bent, kissed my woman's temple and uttered, "See you soon."

"Okay, Blue." She tried to send me a smile, only it was

forced. Her mind was elsewhere, and I couldn't blame her.

Once they were out of earshot, I said to Talon and Griz, "Let's get in there before your woman kills the bitch. We need answers. I want to know who I need to take down for all this shit to stop."

"Let's do it then."

CHAPTER SIXTEEN

BLUE

*a*s soon as I opened the door, we could hear Hell Mouth yelling at the top of her lungs. I spotted her in front of a desk Vi sat at. I didn't expect to see Julian standing beside her, but there he was with his hands on his hips and a glare in his eyes.

"Let me fuckin' in there, Vi," Hell Mouth snapped. She leaned her hands on the desk and forced her body forward so she was closer to a calm-looking Violet.

"Again, Barbie, not happening," she said in a tone which showed she didn't care Deanna was all up in her grill.

"Darlin'," Griz called.

She spun to her man and glared. "Don't you start. Did

you not hear, Grady? That bitch in there," she pointed to the hall, where the interrogation room was, "was gonna sell her own sister. Sell her!" she screamed. "She needs a goddamn, motherfuckin' lesson delivered to her, and I'm the one who's gonna beat the ever-lovin' shit out of her."

Griz had a small smile on his face. Anyone could see he was proud to call her his woman. If it came to a beat-down, she was ready to get the show on the road.

"Cool it for a while, Hell Mouth," I started. "We need answers first, and *then* you can have your beat-down."

Her smile was pure fuckin' joy.

"I'm watching," Julian piped in with a tone I'd never heard him use. He was angry. "No one gets away with hurting my buttercup."

"Just send Butch out here when you go in," Violet ordered.

Talon and Vi had been through some shit in the past, so it was fucking great to see her have her brother's back in these types of situations. What also helped was the fact our club didn't deal with illegal shit any longer, which helped her change her attitude. And Wildcat. It was actually funny how that all worked out, that she was working for Vi before Talon claimed her. It was Zara who brought them back together, which made Talon love her that much more. Though, his love for his woman was stronger than anything. No one would want to cause shit there, or they'd be in a hell of a lot of trouble.

Just like I felt with Clarinda.

I started off down the hall with Talon, Griz, Deanna and Julian following. With a swift knock on a steel door to the back of the hall, I waited for a reply.

"In." I opened the door and saw big-arse Butch sitting on a chair facing backward as he stared down Amy. She was tied down to a chair with a smug smile on her face. There was nothing else in the room. "I'll leave you to it," Butch said and left, closing the door behind him.

I moved to the chair he'd just vacated, turned it around and sat. Talon stood on one side of me, Griz was leaning against the door and Hell Mouth stood just behind me with Julian.

Amy rolled her eyes and then looked from one face to another; her eyes landed back on me, and then she asked, "You come to welcome me to the family? Seems you've taken a liking to my sister." She then threw her head back and laughed.

"Bitch," Talon hissed, and her eyes went to him. "You need to shut the fuck up, or Hell Mouth will make you."

"Hell Mouth?" she questioned.

"Yeah." Deanna glared.

Amy turned to her and then laughed again. "Oh, I'm really scared." She snorted and added, "Not like precious little Clarinda will let anything happen to her sister."

"That's because she isn't a raging psycho like you are," Julian said.

"What's the fag doing in here anyway?"

"Shut the fuck up," I growled. Her gaze quickly turned

to me. "You need to answer all our questions, or I will make your life fuckin' Hell. Do you understand me?"

She scoffed. "My life is *already* Hell. You couldn't make it worse."

My upper lip rose off my teeth. "I can and I fuckin' will. You won't know when it will happen, you won't know *how* it will happen, but I'll be there watching, waiting for my right moment, and that moment will be when you least expect it. Maybe even when you've finally fuckin' found a happy place, and then I'll rip everything away from you. So much so, you won't want to continue living."

The room fell silent.

Amy's eyes never strayed from mine, and I never once looked away. I hoped to Christ she understood I was dead serious about it, because I was.

"What do you want to know?" she asked.

"Was all this just your plan? Were you the mastermind for all this crap?"

She rolled her eyes. "In a way, yes, but then again, Henry was beside me along for the ride. He was the one who organised the kill on our parents."

"You sick bitch," Hell Mouth uttered, shaking her head.

"Fuck you. You don't know what I've had to do."

"What? Get stuck on crack? Get in the wrong crowd? Not being goddamn smart enough to pull yourself out of it for your family? You obviously took the easy way every time. Hell, Henry must have a big dick for him to pull your strings and get you to do what he wants."

"Shut the fuck up!" she screamed and rocked in her seat, shaking her head back and forth.

Holy motherfucking shit. She was crazy.

"Tell us where we can find Henry, Amy. Tell us how we can get all this to stop," I ordered.

With her head bent, her eyes to the floor, she laughed. "You can't do anything."

"Maybe we can make a deal, you for them to back off."

She looked up and smirked. "He won't take it. He knows you won't kill me. He'll get his boys to wait and grab me when the time is right. I'll be sorry to see my sister die, but it's what he'll do. I can't stop them now." She shrugged, pulling on her restraints. "And why would I? I'll be rich then, so I won't care."

I stood slowly, and her eyes widened.

There was a knock on the door.

We all turned to it, and I was surprised to see Wildcat standing on the other side of the door. She smiled into the room, but then glared at Amy when her eyes spotted her as she walked inside.

"Ah… Zara, this ain't your type of thing," Deanna said.

"Oh, I know. But Clary brought up something while we were having a coffee." She looked to Amy and asked, "Clary said she has an eye appointment coming up soon, but she's unsure of the address. I came on by to grab it for her."

We all waited.

That was when Amy started laughing once a-fucking-gain.

"Damn, she is the most stupid, gullible person out there."

"What are you talking about?" Zara asked.

That was what I wanted to know, and I was glad she voiced the question, because I was about ready to slap Amy's stupid head off her fuckin' shoulders.

"When she was passed out in the hospital after the fire, I overheard the doctors talking." She smiled to herself.

"And?" Julian snapped.

"They said she'd recover her sight with an operation and some time."

Zara gasped, her hand flying to her mouth. Deanna cursed, and a growl filled my lungs and rolled out of me.

"Y-you mean Clary will regain full sight if she has an operation?" Julian clarified.

Amy chuckled. "Yeah, but I couldn't have that. I needed her to rely on me, become dependent on me."

"What about all her other appointments?" Talon barked.

Another chuckle as she shook her head. "Fake. I took her to a house where Henry's guy would pretend to be a doctor."

Closing my eyes, I fought for control.

My woman had lived five years with no sight and she didn't have to. Fuck.

A slap echoed through the room. I opened my eyes in hope it was Deanna going crazy, but instead, I found Wildcat standing over Amy. "How could you?" she yelled and slapped her again. "She's your own sister." Another slap. "You have no heart." Another slap.

"Can I join in, or should I stop her?" Hell Mouth asked.

I shrugged. I was still in fucking shock to see Wildcat going... well, wild.

"Kitten," Talon called calmly with a smile upon his face.

"In a minute," she snapped back to her man, and then slapped Amy again. "This will stop. You deserve to die for what you did to your sister." She spun around and pointed at Talon and then Amy. "Shoot her."

He chuckled. "Kitten."

"No, shoot her, or I will."

"Hot damn, woman." Deanna grinned.

I felt my pants being tugged, and then in the next second, the room was filled with a gun being fired. Talon was on Wildcat, Griz tackled Deanna to the ground and I looked to the person holding the gun as Amy's scream followed next.

"Julian," I said quietly and held out my hand for my gun. I glanced at Amy because he wouldn't take his eyes from her. She was doubled over in pain, but the only blood I saw was pouring out of her shin. "Julian," I tried again.

"Has everyone in this room gone fuckin' crazy?" Hell Mouth yelled from the floor. Griz climbed off her and helped her stand.

"Honey?" Zara said to her man as she searched his face for something. When he nodded, she gave him a peck on the lips and walked to Julian. "Hey, slugger. You took all the fun away. I wanted to shoot her." Still, Julian said nothing. I wasn't sure where he was. "Julian," Zara tried again. She stepped in front of him as Amy's cries of pain turned into whimpers. She deserved more.

The door was flung open, and in came Vi with Butch just behind her. "Please, in all that's mighty, tell me we do not have a body to clean up?" She stepped around Griz and Deanna to see Amy breathing and alive in the chair. She gazed at her leg, closed her eyes and sighed. "Fuck."

Vi quieted the complaint which was on her lips when she took in Zara's worried gaze. Zara reached her hand up to cover Julian's cheek. "Julian, honey, where are you right now? Come back to us," she pleaded.

Suddenly, he blinked hard and focused on Zara's face. "Family should be a safe haven," he whispered.

"Yes, yes they should," Zara encouraged.

"But she didn't make it safe for Clary." His bottom lip wobbled. Holy shit. It was obvious something in Julian's past had caused him to snap.

"No, she didn't."

"That was wrong. So many wrong things can happen in families. So many bad things can happen. So many hurtful things. My buttercup doesn't need that."

Zara's eyes welled. I wondered if she knew what was happening right then in Julian's mind.

"She doesn't, Julian. Which is why she has us now. She has a new family, like you do. She'll heal with time, like you have, and we'll all take care of each other."

His thoughts took him to one last place, and when he blinked hard again, he gave her what she needed—a small smile.

"We will, won't we?" he prompted.

"Yes." She smiled up at him, and then took him in for a hug. Another shock for the fucking day was when Deanna, with tears in her eyes, walked up to them and joined the huddle.

"Y-you may be too late to take care of her," Amy croaked. We all turned to her. "He's still watching her. He'd never take his eyes from his target, especially when they cost so much."

My eyes widened and I spun to Talon. "Who's with her?"

"Killer, Ivy, and I called Billy, Tame and Whip to come in. They should be there."

I needed to be sure myself. I needed my eyes on my woman and now. They all cleared a path and I ran out of the room, down the hall and outta the front office with a fire lit under my feet, my heart beating double-time in a panicked state.

I ran down the footpath toward the bakery like a mad man. I was in the door in the next second, just as mother-fucking Henry was pulling a gun out and ordering Clary to get to her feet and come to him or he'd shoot up the room. The stupid dick hadn't registered I was in the store, but he soon found out when I was on his back. We fell to the ground in a heap; thank fuck his gun fell from his hand as he tried to protect his fall. Screams filled the room, and people ran for safety out the door. I ripped Henry's arms behind his back and growled, "Stay."

"Brother?" I looked behind me to see Tame and Whip standing there. I climbed to my knees off Henry and ordered them to take him to Vi's.

Once they were out the door, my eyes sought out my woman. She was in the far corner cradled in Ivy's arms as Killer stood in front of them both. A huge sigh of relief left my lungs.

We had them.

Fuck.

It was over.

CHAPTER SEVENTEEN

TWO HOURS LATER

CLARINDA

*M*y man had saved the day. I never thought I'd feel so much fear, but I had when Henry showed in the bakery and people started shouting there was a gun. When he ordered me up, I was prepared to do anything, because my fear was for the other people in the shop. Only, Ivy had told me no and held me close to her.

After it all, Blue took me from the bakery, back to Vi's and straight into a car. He'd told me I'd had enough excitement for the day and was taking me back to the compound, to our room.

He had something else on his mind, though.

I could only hope he would share once we were safe and sound.

However, as soon as the door was closed and I heard the lock slip into place, all talking was out the window. He pulled me into his arms, and in an urgent need, we went wild. I think it was because we both needed that reassurance we were alive and safe.

Running my hands under his tee, I lifted it, and his hands left me for a second. Once I had his shirt off and flung it sideways, he returned the favour and quickly removed mine. My bra was next, and then as his hands roamed my breasts, back and stomach, we kissed. Still, it wasn't enough.

Trailing my hands down his defined abdomen, I came to his jeans. I flicked the button open and slid down the fly. My hand glided in to find he wasn't wearing any boxers like he usually did, so I gripped him. He pulled back and moaned loudly.

"Fuck, sugar. I need you so bad," he growled as he rested his forehead against mine.

"Then take me," I whispered.

"Christ, yes."

He picked me up, and I wound my legs around his waist and my arms around his neck. With a hand threaded through my hair, he brought my head down so he could claim my lips again in a passionate kiss.

He took a couple of steps as we kissed, and then bent, my back hitting the mattress. He stepped back, his warmth leaving me. I really wanted to have it back and for it to never leave. I reached my hand out to him.

"Hang on, sugar." I heard his pants hit the floor, and then his fingers were at my jeans. He worked them undone and slipped them from my legs, taking my panties with them.

I reached out again to his shadowed form and uttered, "Blue."

"Fuck, baby," he groaned. That was when I knew he was just standing above me, looking down. I smiled, because it definitely sounded like he liked what he saw.

Which had me wishing I was able to see him.

"Scoot up, sugar, and roll onto your belly."

Grinning, I did as I was told, because I was so ready for what was to happen next. Climbing onto the bed, he took hold of my ankles and separated my legs. I gasped as he ran his hands up each leg, and then I whimpered when he teased my pussy with a finger on each side. He massaged the tops of my thighs and I wiggled down a bit, wanting him to touch me between my legs.

"Patience, sugar," Blue growled low, lust riding his voice, and it was wonderful to hear.

"No. Please, Blue."

"Aw, hell, baby." The warmth of his chest hit my back,

and he leaned over me as he slid two fingers straight inside my pussy. I arched and was rewarded with a kiss to my temple. "My sugar is so wet and ready. Christ, baby, I love your pussy."

"Hmm," was my only reply, because he'd just arched his fingers and hit the right spot. His chest left my back and I felt his lips trail down my spine. Then he kissed my behind, only to bite it in the next second, causing me to squeal. "Blue."

His took his finger from within me and I heard a sucking sound. Oh, God, was he licking my juices from his fingers?

He hissed and then answered my thoughts. "Sweet as sugar; that's what you taste like."

He was over me once more. "Spread farther, baby," he said. I shifted my legs wider. The tip of his cock at my entrance, he asked, "You ready for me to claim your body, sugar?"

"Yes," I moaned.

"Jesus, you sound sweet, too," he groaned and pushed forward. His cock entered slowly; my walls gripped him all the way. It was Heaven. "Fuck, I'll never get bored of your body, of you."

"Oh God, Blue. Fuck me, please."

"You want it hard?" he asked.

I did; I was growing impatient. He wasn't moving, only embedded inside me. Even though I loved the feel of him filling me to the brink, I wanted more. "Please,

please, fuck me hard, Blue."

"Yeah, baby?"

"Yes," I growled.

He chuckled, only to stop as he withdrew from my depths and surged forward.

"God, yes!" I yelled as he kept fucking me hard, pounding into me over and over.

His hand clamped into my hair, ripping my head back so he could lean over me more, and as he claimed my body, he took my mouth, as well. It was all so overwhelming I instantly came. I cried out around his mouth, my pussy's drenched walls milking his cock.

"Damn, ah, fuck yes. Your pussy feels so good," he moaned. "Fuckin' beautiful. I love seeing you come, sugar, but you got another one in you yet," he ordered as he continued moving inside me.

"Blue, it's too much," I whimpered and gripped the bed sheets.

"No, Clary, it isn't. You can do it, sugar. Just feel it. Feel my cock driving into you."

"I do. Oh, hell, I do, Blue."

"Yeah, baby," he growled. "My woman feels me." His chest rested fully on top of me. I felt his hand sneak under us and then his finger was at my clit, teasing it.

"Oh, oh... yes, Blue, yes," I cried out.

"That's it, fuck yeah," he said into my ear, where he bit the lobe next, pulling another orgasm from my body.

"Shit, yes, yes, your walls are clamping around me,

baby. Fuck, I'm gonna come. You're making me come, sugar. Yeahhhh," he groaned.

We both breathed hard as we came back down to Earth. Blue moaned as he flopped off my back and onto the bed beside me. "Damn, woman," he sighed.

Giggling, I rolled into him and put my head on his chest, feeling some of his seed slip from my body. "Is it time to talk now?" I asked.

He burst out laughing. "Shit. Give me a while, and then we'll talk."

"Okay." I yawned and snuggled in deeper to him.

I was more than content to do just that. My sister was locked away; her friends were, as well. I was safe and in the arms of the man I loved. *Talking can definitely wait*, I thought as I drifted off to sleep.

A KNOCK DRIFTED into my sleepy daze, and the bed shifted as Blue climbed out. I hoped he'd think to put some clothes on first, but I was too sleepy to say anything.

The door swished open, and then I heard a gasp. "Oh, um, you, uh...." I stifled my giggle; I had never heard Julian stutter before.

"Hey," Blue clipped. "Eyes up here, man."

"Well now, what do you expect when you flaunt it in front of me? It's like dangling a... oops." He laughed.

"Julian," he snapped. "Dammit, man, eyes at my face, for fuck's sake. Now, tell me what you're doing here."

"Do you know how hard that is?" He burst out laughing again and gasped for breath. I hid under the blankets and laughed quietly. "I don't mean you; you're not hard… well, not that I know of. If you just removed your hand—"

"Julian," Blue barked.

"Right, right. I came to see how my buttercup was. But I can tell you've taken good care of her." Blue grunted. "Did you tell her what happened?" he asked in a whisper. However, it was Julian, and he loved to be loud, so his whisper was not exactly a whisper.

The room was silent for a second, and then Blue said, "No, not yet."

"Maybe give her the bad news first… you know… bang, and then tell her the good news. Do you want me to stay?"

Bad news?

"Nah, man, it's cool. I'll sort it all out. How you doin' anyway?"

Clothes were shifted; I think Julian shrugged. Why would Blue be asking him how he was doing?

"M'kay, I guess. Do you… do you think she'll hate me?" My heart actually felt like it was shattering at hearing Julian speak so sadly. How could he ever think I'd hate him? He helped save me. He had been there for me right at the start. He helped show me there *was* light in life.

"No, Julian. I'm sure if you explained what set you off and that you wanted to protect her, she'll get it."

"Thanks, Blue," Julian said with a smile in his voice, and then he added, "You know, I could stay and keep you entertained until she wakes."

"Jesus Christ, you just don't stop. How does Mattie handle you?"

"Oh, he knows what a flirt I am. It's harmless, though. I just love seeing the reactions. It's priceless. However, my Mattie also knows how to keep me satisfied in bed. Why, just this morning—"

"Fuck. Goodbye, Julian!" Blue yelled and slammed the door.

I flipped the sheet back with a smile on my face as I knew Blue would be turning to face the bed.

"You heard all that?"

"Yes. Were you really standing there with nothing but your hand covering your... bit?"

His footsteps approached, and then his weight was on top of me. My legs spread to accommodate him, and he thrust forward, his hard cock sliding against my folds and clit.

"I take that as a yes," I laughed. "Julian would have loved the show. I just know I'll be hearing about it later."

Blue growled low. "That guy... sometimes I just don't know how to take him. But I do know he would do anything to take care of my woman, so I guess he's all right in my eyes."

My smiled faded. "Blue, what did he mean? Why would he think I could hate him?"

"Shit, I was hoping for a little play before we got serious. Do you wanna get dressed before we talk?"

"No."

"Okay, sugar." He climbed off to sit next to me. Blue dragged my body up with the sheet wrapped around me and placed me in his lap. His arms wound around my waist.

"I've got two things to tell you, and those two things will blow your mind, baby. So be prepared, okay?"

With the serious tone in his voice, I didn't think I could get prepared. I knew what he was about to say was going to change things; I just didn't know how. Still, I said, "Yes, Blue."

"Hell, there ain't no easy way to bring you in slow, so I'm just gonna say it." When I nodded, he took a deep breath and said, "When I went into Vi's office, I found Deanna and Julian already in there. They wanted a word with your sister, and because I can be an arse, and for what she had done to my woman, I allowed them to come back, because I thought Hell Mouth would give Amy a piece of her mind. She did...but it wasn't her who shocked the shit out of me."

"Who did?"

"Wildcat came down to tell us about you havin' a

doctor's appointment comin' up soon." I nodded, and he continued, "Right, well, when your sister said some shit, people started to lose it."

"What did she say?"

"We'll get to that in a second. Clary, baby, you have touched so many hearts in such a fuckin' small amount of time, and because you have, we all saw red. I was about to rip through her when Wildcat started slapping her and yellin' at her, tellin' her she never deserved you as a sister. It was fuckin' beautiful. I have never in the years I've known Zara seen her go off like that. She was all momma-bear-protective."

Oh... wow. Was it bad I liked Zara beating on my sister for my sake? I felt terrible for not hating the thought... but I didn't. If anything, it warmed me. Did that make me a bad human being?

"You okay so far, Clary? We *are* talking about your sister here."

"I know, babe. But... she was never a good sister, Blue. She was going to sell me," I whispered into the room.

My sister was going to sell me.

That was something I would never get over.

"Good, I'm glad you said that. Because I think that, plus the shit your sister said in that room, set something off in Julian, and it was bad, baby. He lost it, and for a while, we couldn't get him back. But, Clary, when he lost it, he took my gun from my holster and shot your sister in the shin."

My breath left my body so suddenly I coughed to try and get some air back in. Blue sat me up straight and rubbed my back. "Clary, baby, are you okay?"

"I-I...." I put my hand up for a moment, indicating he needed to wait while I composed myself. In that time, thoughts ran wild in my mind.

Julian, sweet, caring Julian shot my sister in the shin.

He picked up a gun and shot my sister.

Oh God, I hope he's okay.

What on Earth could have been going through his mind at the time? It would *have* to have been big for that to happen. I couldn't even imagine Julian holding a gun, let alone shooting it. I needed to see him, talk to him.

My eyes widened when I came to one conclusion.

I hadn't even been worried what sort of pain my sister was in, or even if she was okay. All my thoughts were on Julian.

And that said a lot to me.

It was terrible to say, but if she'd been shot dead, I think I would have had a different reaction. Then again, after finding out what she had done to me, what she was behind, even our parents' death, the love I had for my sibling seemed to have disappeared.

I have never known a human being to be so horrid.

Only now I did, and it was my own sister.

"Sugar?"

Turning toward him, I said, "I'm okay."

His body jolted, like I had shocked him. "Are you sure?"

"Yes. I'll have a talk with Julian."

"Baby?"

"I need him to know I don't care what he did. I know in a way he did it for me, and in a way, for whatever reason, he did it for himself. But shooting someone can cause a lot of trauma. I need to see if he's okay and tell him I could never hate such a wonderful man."

Suddenly, I was brought tightly to Blue's chest. "Goddamn, you are fuckin' perfect. I was so scared, baby, so scared you would run to her side to see if she was okay, and then somehow she'd manipulate you into staying away from us, from me. But I can see now you see your bitch of a sister for what she truly is."

I nodded against his chest. "A horrid piece of work. Someone I no longer want in my life. Someone I never want to see or talk to again." I pulled back so he could see my face. "I need to move forward now. I need to get my life back on track and learn how to live with this disability on my own. Not that I don't want you around, but—"

Blue's hand fell over my mouth.

My eyes narrowed up at him. What was he doing?

"There's something else I need to tell you." He removed his hand and wrapped me up in his arms once again. "You know how I told you something your sister said set Zara off?"

"Of course."

"Well, fuck, baby, she set you up right at the start."

"What do you mean?" I questioned. My body knew I wasn't going to like what Blue was about to say; my heart beat faster and my body shivered. I bit my bottom lip and waited for his answer.

"Clary, she took you out of the hospital because she overheard a doctor saying you would be able to have your sight back if you got a heap of rest and an operation."

"No," I hissed.

"Yeah, sugar," he said and ran his hand up and down my arm. "The doctor you were seeing was a fake, one of her fella's men. Baby, we'll get you to a real one. We'll sort this out, and then, *then* you'll be able to see again."

A sob tore through me. My hands went over my face as tears poured out and cries wrecked my body.

"Fuck, Clary?"

She lied to me. That whole time. Five fucking years, I'd been blind and didn't have to be. Five fucking years of Hell, living with her. Five fucking years of my life, wasted, because of her.

Five years.

Oh, God.

Wiping my hands over my face, I moved from Blue's hold and climbed off the bed, holding the sheet to my body.

"Clary, baby?"

185

"Blue," I choked out. My hands went around my waist. I didn't know what to do, what to think or even how to think.

Five years.

"Hell, baby," Blue said softly, and I felt him stand behind me. He turned me, and I buried my face against his bare shoulder. I had forgotten he was naked.

"I'll be able to see," I mumbled against him.

"Yeah, sugar," he replied with a smile.

"I'll be able to look at you, *see* you, babe."

He chuckled. "You may not like what you see."

Pulling my head back, I frowned up at him. "It has never mattered to me what you look like, Blue. Never. What matters is the way you've been with me. Since my parents passed, I have never felt warmth. I have never felt wanted and I've never felt safe. Not until you. No matter what, Blue, I'll always want you, because you have been my *everything* since the first time I sensed you in that café."

"Christ, sugar," he growled and rested his forehead against mine. "You're also my everything. It may have taken me a while to see it, because at first, I thought you were playing me. But when I did, that first night I held you in my arms in this bed, my eyes opened wide and took it all in. Now you're the light in my heart which guides me to wherever you are."

My heart melted. Never had I ever heard such sweet words.

"Tell me I can fuck you now," Blue said in a low, seductive tone.

"Soon—"

"Clary," he warned. "I need to have you."

"And you will, soon. I need to talk to Julian first."

"Christ, I better get some clothes on for that."

CHAPTER EIGHTEEN

CLARINDA

*A*fter we were dressed, Blue walked with me from the compound and across the road to Mattie and Julian's house. He knocked on the door, and within a second, it opened.

"I hoped you would come tonight," Mattie said. "He's been really worried about you, Clary."

I nodded. "He won't have to now. Can I talk to him for a bit?" Blue, with a hand on my lower back, guided me up the last step. I heard the door close behind us and felt Mattie at my other side.

"Honey, I hope you don't mind me saying, but I've got to know, for my guy's sake. Are you going to go easy on him? He regrets what he did, honey, but he's concerned he ruined any type of relationship you both had. If you're here to tell him that... I can't have it. I need to protect him in every way I can."

Reaching out to take hold of his hand on my arm, I said, "You don't need to worry; I'm here to ease any unwelcome thoughts he has. There is no way I could ever hate your man. He means too much to me."

"Jesus, thank you," he uttered, and then hugged me tight. "I'll go get him. Blue can take you into the kitchen, and we'll be in there in a second."

"Thanks." I smiled.

I sat in a kitchen chair, Blue standing close at my back. His hand was on my shoulder, gently rubbing his thumb over my collarbone.

"You get this done real quick, sugar."

Snorting, I said, "Blue."

"No. Real quick," he growled.

"We'll see."

Footsteps approached. From the smell, Julian and his citrus scent walked into the kitchen first, and then Mattie, with his ocean-scented body.

"B-buttercup?"

My lips trembled; he sounded so troubled. "Julian," I whispered and held out my arms. His quick steps approached, and he was on his knees in front of me with his arms around my waist. I leaned over him and hugged his back, sliding one hand up and down. "Everything is fine," I whispered as tears filled my eyes. "Nothing you could do can stop me from caring about you. Nothing."

He nodded into my lap. My jeans felt wet, and that was how I knew he was crying silently in my arms.

Sniffling, I asked the others, "Give us a minute?" Blue leaned over and kissed my neck, and then I heard him walk out of the room with Mattie. As Julian cried, I told him, "After what Blue told me this afternoon, I never thought I could hate a person so much. But I do. My own sister took away five years of my life. The only enjoyment I got from it was when I went to the library and this guy came up to annoy me. Though, he annoyed me in a way, I learned later, also touched my heart. He touched it in a way which made an imprint. He touched it in a way which had me wishing I was a part of his family, instead of my own. Julian, you are important to me, so no matter what I can forgive and forget what you did, because you did it to protect me, and that means so much to me." I stopped, licked my lips and then said, "But, honey, from what I was told, there was something else at play in that room, and I want you to know I'm here for you if you ever need to talk. I'm here to protect you, too, in any way I can, like you have for me. I'm here for you always."

That was when I found out Julian, the one man who I'd never expect to have a story which was so scary and sad, did. He filled me in on a part of his life which could have cracked any man under all the pressure, especially after what he went through. But then he told me about what brought him through it all—Mattie. Like Julian had been there for me at the library, Mattie had been there for Julian, and it made me love Mattie all that much more, because if it wasn't for him, I wouldn't have had my safe haven in the worst five years of my life.

Blue had been my everything.

But Julian had also been there along with him.

My world, my life had changed for the better, because of those two people, so I knew I would do anything for them both.

It was after I had finished a cup of coffee Julian had made when the front door banged open. "Girls' night, get the fuck out!" Deanna yelled. She stomped through the house, heading toward the kitchen.

"Ah, hell no. I'm taking my woman back to the compound," Blue said on a growl, his heavy footsteps following Deanna's.

"Get stuffed. I was told a girls' night may be needed, so I'm here. Hey, arse-face, and... um, Clary," Deanna said as she came to a stop somewhere near the kitchen door. Her blurred outline showed she was just inside the door-way. There was another behind her, so it was hard to tell.

"Sugar, let's go," Blue hissed.

"She ain't leaving, Mr…"

"Skies," I supplied.

"Fuck," Blue uttered.

The room was silent for a second, and then giggles from Julian and loud laughter from Deanna broke through. "Oh my God, your last name is Skies?" Deanna teased and then laughed again.

Whoops. I guess no one knew.

"Deanna Drake. Next time, don't leave all the carrying to just us," Zara's pissed voice sounded from the front room.

"Us? Who in the fuck is us?" Blue snapped. "Oh Christ, no. My woman is not drinking that shit, and she sure as shit ain't drinking with you lot. That's when trouble starts."

"Come on, Blue. I'm new to the group, so I can promise to keep them under control," Ivy's sweet, light voice said from the living room.

I had to laugh. My poor man and I were expecting to have a quiet night together. It was already night anyway; I'd asked Blue on our way over. Earlier, we had slept for two hours, so it would have to be about nine pm when Deanna charged through the door.

"Sugar, up now. We're going."

"Blue."

"No, no fuckin' way."

"Listen here, hard arse," Deanna started. "If you can

answer one question with the right answer, you can take your woman and root like rabbits all night long."

"Fine," he hissed through clenched teeth.

"Has Clary in any way, shape or form totally lost it about everything that has happened?"

I bit my bottom lip and looked to the ground. I hadn't. Okay, I had a little. But had it been enough? At the time, I shoved it back, because I knew I didn't have time for it. Julian needed some reassuring, so I went there first.

So, did I still need to lose it?

I wasn't sure of the answer.

"No," Blue uttered.

"Dude," Deanna sighed sadly. "She needs to. I know, and Zara knows, she needs to get drunk, scream, yell, cry and rant, and she needs her girls with her along for the ride. You can stay, by all means, but it's gonna get crazy. Because not only are we going to talk about her bitch of a sister, but there's going to be words about our men, their cocks and how good they give it. Are you ready for that?"

"Um…" I began. "I've never been drunk before."

"Holy hot men in tights. Surely you are jesting with me, buttercup?" Julian asked from where he sat across from me.

"I'm not joking."

"Well, shit," Deanna laughed. "You're gonna love this, and then your man will love us when he reaps the benefits from having drunk, wild sex with his woman."

I gasped. Deanna never held anything back; she bared

all and didn't care what anyone thought. I actually admired that in her, except when I was turning red from embarrassment.

"Fuck," Blue complained. "Okay, I guess we'll both get what we want, *eventually*."

"Blue," I snapped.

"What, sugar?"

"You can't say things like that."

"What the fuck, baby? Hell Mouth just stood there and told me you're gonna talk about my cock and how good I give it to you, and you want me to keep it clean?"

"That's different." I shrugged.

"Hell, I'm gonna need reinforcements. I'm ringing the other men. I'll need a fuckin' heap of help for this night," he said, and I listened to his retreating footsteps, which walked right out the front door.

"Let's get this party started," Deanna shouted.

Somewhere, I heard Mattie sigh and ask, "Why did I call them?" I had to smile. There was so much love in their family, and it bloomed my heart into a full flower, because I was now a part of it.

A hand touched my arm, and I jumped slightly. "Sorry, honey," Ivy said. "But I was just wondering if you're at all scared about this like me."

"Maybe just a little," I whispered.

"Oh, don't worry, you two. We've only had one incident on a drinking night," Zara said.

"What's that?" Ivy asked what I was thinking.

"Our little momma bear there got tasered and kidnapped. But in the end, it was all fine and dandy. The man who kidnapped her is Vi's fella."

"Oh my God," Ivy breathed. Again, she seemed to voice my thoughts exactly.

CHAPTER NINETEEN

BLUE

*F*uck. *Fuck. Fuck.*

Why in the hell did I agree to this again? Oh, right, I was gonna get drunk, wild sex from my woman. At least *that* I was looking forward to, but this... listening to this, was fucking Hell. No, it was probably worse than Hell.

It was more like dressing in drag and going to a gay bar with Julian.

Still, in one way, I was glad to be there so I could care for my woman when she was bawling her eyes out over her fucking bitch sister. She kept repeating over and over that she'd wasted five fucking years with her. I felt useless when she wouldn't stop crying, so then I felt like whipping my dick out, going for a surprised reaction and to change the sad mood.

That was until Zara pried me away from my woman's arms and told me to let her have time, to let her run through her emotions. So, I did, and I was fucking glad I did, because honestly, it would help the healing process.

I didn't know how women knew what each other needed, and I hated to admit Hell Mouth was sure as fuck right. My woman yelled, screamed, cried, and yelled some more. Then, like a goddamn crazy lady, her mood would shift and she'd be laughing, clapping, and singing with glee that she was going to see again.

My whole brain was feeling sick from all the whiplash emotions running through the house.

"Christ, we must love these women," Talon growled after hearing Wildcat informing her posse that when she was still breastfeeding, one night while she was riding her man, her boobs were so full she ended up squirting milk all over him. Griz and I looked to each other and burst out laughing. "Just wait, bastards." Talon smiled.

"Griz and I bought a Kama Sutra book," Deanna announced.

"Jesus," Griz hissed.

"How's that going for you, dicksicle?" Julian asked.

I had never heard so many dirty pet names in my whole life, and that bloody said something, being a biker and all. But Julian's mouth was worse than all the bikers combined, *plus* Hell Mouth. There were names such as:

fanny-fingerer, fishlips, cock-choker, cum-face, cock-gobbler, turkey-slapper, clit-flicker, scrotum-sucker, muff-diver, cunt-breath, and fuck-face.

Christ, the list could go on and on, but they were fucked up enough to hear.

Hell Mouth sighed deeply. "Terrible. Griz is useless in bed."

My eyes widened. Griz was out of his seat in the living room in seconds, and he stomped into the kitchen. "What the fuck you mean by that, woman? You didn't complain when I was giving it to you hard this morning against the wall. You came hard like fuckin' always."

"Babe, I was just seeing if you were listening."

All the women then burst out laughing.

"Jesus Christ," Griz grumbled as he stalked back into the living room and took his spot back on the couch, next to Talon. I was sitting in a chair beside that. "Why didn't we go out like Mattie did? They couldn't have gotten into too much damn trouble."

"Mathew was going to his mum's house. Did you wanna visit Nancy, too?" Talon questioned.

A shudder ran through us all. We liked the woman good enough, but there were only so many times I liked to be hugged or have my arse pinched.

"Do you ladies want to hear all about Blue in bed?"

"Clary," I yelled. "We're leaving now."

"Just a minute, babe," she called, and then started to whisper to the group. I was actually kinda scared.

"Glad you have it now, brother?" Talon asked. I turned to him and smiled.

"Jealous, so many damn times, but now I know why all those times weren't it for me. It was because I was meant to wait for one special woman, and that woman is in that kitchen shooting the shit with your women. She was meant for me. She was made for me and to be able to handle the shit she has and come out strong on the other side to be able to handle me." I laughed to myself as I leaned forward to grab my beer bottle off the coffee table. I sat back in the chair and added, "She was even made to fit with everyone already in our family. She's fuckin' perfect."

I looked up in time to see a female form run at me. I had just enough time to move the bottle out to the left before I had my woman straddling my waist and her hands tangled in my hair.

"Thank Christ that worked, or I would have made a fool of myself." She giggled. "But Ivy pointed me in the right way, because I wanted to run to my man and tell him to take me home to fuck me stupid." Her drunk smile lit up her face.

I chuckled. "I guess you just heard what I said?"

"Oh, yeah, babe, and I want to show you how perfect I think you are by being naked in the next few seconds, and sucking you like you've never been sucked before."

Holy motherfucking shit.

I just knew she was going to regret saying that shit in

front of people, but Christ, my dick just bounced up like it was a dog which had been called by its master.

Placing the beer on the ground, I stood with my woman in my arms and announced to the room, "We're outta here." Laughter and catcalls sounded, but I ignored them all and walked to the door as my woman attacked my neck with her mouth and tongue. Opening the door, I stepped out just as Killer was coming up the walkway.

He looked up and started chuckling. "Good night?"

"You could say that, brother. Good luck in there. You're gonna need it."

His eyes narrowed. "Shit, how drunk are they?"

"Gone."

Clary unlocked her mouth from my neck to whine, "Blue, why aren't we naked yet?"

Killer smiled but shook his head. He continued up the way and I heard him open the door, and then Ivy yelled, "My man's here!"

The whole way across the road and into the compound, Clary kept attacking me, from one side of my neck to the other, and then my lips. I gave her the attention she was after by kissing her back, but I still had to keep an eye open to see where we were heading, or we'd be flat on the floor.

She moaned around my mouth and rubbed her sweet body up and down mine. Her hot centre slid over my cock, teasing it more to life. I was already pretty hard having my woman maul me like she was. I had never seen

Clary so aggressive before. All I knew was that it was a huge bloody turn-on, and I was already thinking of the next time I could get her drunk.

Still, even normal sex was outta this world with my woman.

I just hoped I'd last more than five fucking seconds; she had me that worked up. I could easily blow my load already.

At least we made it safely to our room. I had the door closed before she climbed off me and quickly stripped outta her clothes. I was stunned she moved so fast. I was still dressed when she came at me again.

She pouted and said, "You're not naked." Her hands ran over my body, fixing that problem. She knocked me in the head when she pulled my tee from my body, and she nearly dragged my dick from my body as she gripped it when she was discarding me of my jeans and boxers.

I'd never had to protect myself during sex so much.

"Babe," she said as she wrapped her arms around my naked waist. "I wanna try wall sex. That sounded like fun. But do you want head first?"

"Sugar, a BJ would be goddamn awesome."

"Yay, I like sucking your dick."

I chuckled. "I'm fuckin' glad you do."

Her hands slid down my legs as she got to her knees in front of me. At the first touch of her hot, wet tongue on the tip of my cock, I hissed. She circled it with her tongue before she opened her mouth, guarding her teeth with her lips as she slowly glided her mouth over my hard erection.

"Damn, sugar," I groaned, my head falling back. The feel of her mouth was driving me insane. I looked back down as she picked up speed, watching as she bobbed her red head up and down on my cock. She worked it like I'd never had before. While sucking, she'd drag her tongue around and around.

She pulled back and worked her way down on the bottom of the shaft to my balls, where she took them in hand and gently tugged them forward to wrap her mouth around both at the same time.

"Holy fuckin' shit," I growled. I bent, slid my hands under her arms and dragged her body up. Turning, I slammed her against the wall, picked up her arse and slid straight into her. Her head fell back and she moaned, only it turned into a purr when I started to move within her tight, drenched pussy.

"Yes, Blue, yes. Oh, God, fuck me harder," she cried.

My balls were already drawing up in my body, and yet I pistoned into her harder and faster. My lips went to her neck; an urge, a need had me sucking on her there, marking her.

She was mine.

Pulling away, I looked to the ceiling and groaned, "Fuck, baby, fuck. I'm gonna come soon."

"Yes, hell, yes, me, too. Me, too."

I wasn't sure if I could wait for her to reach it on

her own, so I took one hand off her arse, pushing her into the wall more, causing her to whimper. Moving back slightly, I brought my hand around and touched her clit.

That was all it took.

She cried out and her walls clamped around my cock just in time before I blew my seed straight into her pulsating pussy. All of it ripped a growl from my chest as I emptied the last of it inside her.

Totally and utterly wiped, I supported my woman in my arms and took her to the bed as she tried to catch her breath.

I was fucking fighting my own body; it seemed to lack a heap of oxygen. For a second, I lay down beside her, resting myself. "Christ," I breathed.

"Tell me about it," she sighed.

"Tomorrow, baby, we're sleeping at my house," I told her as I got out of bed to head to the en-suite. We both needed sleep. It had been a monster of a day, and I didn't think Clary was moving anytime soon.

"You have a house?" I heard her ask.

Laughing as I walked back out of the bathroom with a warm washcloth in my hand, I said, "Yeah, sugar."

"But I thought you lived here."

"No way, baby."

"But... you're always here."

"Sugar," I smiled; she just hadn't caught on yet. "it's because you're here. Until your shit was over, I wasn't leaving you and going to sleep elsewhere. At least now your shit is over."

"Yeah?"

"Yeah, baby. They're both in jail now. They'll have a hearing, but honestly, with the evidence against both of them and with all the fuckin' witnesses, I doubt they'll get out any time soon. And I doubt they'll need you to stand as witness in the courtroom."

"That would be good if I could miss that." She paused for a moment before she whispered into the room, "I don't ever want to see her again, Blue. Is that terrible? She's my sister, and I never want to see her again."

"No, sugar. That ain't terrible. If anything, it's fuckin' sweet for you to even think it's terrible after what she's done to you."

"You're perfect, Blue."

"So are you, Clary. Now, open wide so I can clean you up." She shifted a goddamn centimetre. Laughing, I helped her move her legs farther apart so I could wipe her clean. I threw the washcloths to the floor and laid down next to my woman who moaned, and it didn't sound like a good one. I got back up and went to grab her a glass of water. Crawling back on the bed, I leaned over to kiss her back.

"Blue, I don't feel too well," she whined. I chuckled and kissed her temple. "Hmph, don't touch me," she mumbled into the mattress.

"Sugar, you need some water."

"I'll take it through a drip."

Hell, she was cute.

"I'm never drinking again," she complained one last time, and then started snoring.

Shaking my head and smiling, I put the water on the bedside table. Rearranging her body without her waking, so she was under the sheet instead of on top, I slid in next to her, bringing her back to my front.

Life, right then, could not have been sweeter.

CHAPTER TWENTY

CLARINDA

*T*he following week was magical. When I woke after my first night of drinking, it felt like a rubbish truck had driven over me and dumped all their haul in my mouth. It took me half the day to feel half-normal, and then the other half was spent hiding from everyone when I remembered I nearly raped my man at Julian and Mattie's house.

Still, the night was exactly what I needed.

That was when I remembered Blue saying something about going to his house. I had honestly thought he lived at the compound, but when I thought of when he said he was only sleeping there because I was, I swooned for my man even more.

After putting up with some of his own teasing for the day and finding I had a huge hicky on my neck, I demanded he take me to his house and look after me while I recovered from my drunken night.

He did.

The only thing I wished was that I could see it. Though, it wouldn't be long until I could. When Monday came, Nancy came around to Blue's early and sat with me as I made a call, with my heart beating wildly, to book an appointment with a doctor for the operation I should have had five years before.

I was nervous.

Still, I couldn't wait.

I was ready to see many things.

I was ready to see all my new friends.

And Blue.

Giddy was an understatement when I thought of being able to see my man. I was over-the-moon happy, filled with so much joy.

Blue came with me to my appointment and held my shaking hand as the doctor informed me the operation would be a day procedure in the outpatient's unit, and would go ahead in a week's time. But after it, there would be a period of healing with patches over my eyes. He wasn't sure how long that would take, but he gave us a rough estimate of a week or two. Nothing he said bothered me. If the conclusion was I would be able to see, I didn't care what I would have to go through. The consultant, Mr Wellis, couldn't understand why I didn't have the operation after the accident and I'd come out of the coma. Honestly, I didn't want to go through it all. Blue must have sensed that, because he stated, "Personal issues. We'll just leave it at that."

So I was booked in, and since I was really getting a normal life back, I had to make some other changes in my life, as well.

Blue had come home to his house to find Zara and Ivy with me. We were sitting at the kitchen table, drinking coffee, and Ivy had her laptop with her so we could check out some rental properties around the area. My lawyer had rang that morning with the answer to the question I'd asked him about two days prior. He was allowing the early release on my inheritance for the hospital bills and finding myself a place to settle down in. He was appalled with what I had been through, so he was happy to help me in some way. "Besides," he said, "it's your money in the end anyway. You're just getting it a little early." That was when I asked how much money. He cleared his throat and said, "Two million dollars." I had been standing in Blue's kitchen, leaning against the island bench, but when he said that, my bottom was on the floor. Shocked was definitely an understatement at that point in time.

Anyway, I was sitting with Zara and Ivy as they told me about a few possible choices around the area. I was leaning toward the three-bedroom brick home, and was voicing that when Blue came around the corner and into the kitchen. I knew it because that was when he yelled, "What in the fuck is goin' on?"

Frowning, I asked, "What are you yelling for?"

"Tell me, woman, that you were not just talking about finding a place to live?" he growled deeply. From what I could tell, he was standing in the opening of the doorway with his hands on his hips.

"Well, yeah," I said, puzzled over why he would be pissed about that.

"Are. You. My. Woman?"

I shook my head at him; he was being ridiculous. "Yes, Blue."

"Then why are you looking for somewhere to live?"

"Babe, I need a place to call home."

"And you can't here?" he snapped.

"Blue, you've done so much for me, but I can't live here. We're just getting sorted."

"Clary—"

"No. We need time to date like a normal couple."

"Clary," he hissed.

"Um," Zara started, "I think it's time we leave." She stood, her and Ivy's chairs scraping back on the hardwood floor.

"But I thought you two were helping me?" I asked.

Ivy's rose scent wafted closer as she leaned over and whispered, "Honey, I don't think you'll need to look for a place."

My head shot back. "Why?"

"For fuck's sake," Blue barked. "Your women get it, so why can't you? Let me just tell you. You'll be living here with me."

"Blue—"

"Clary, are you my woman?"

"Yes," I snapped.

"Then my woman stays by my side, where I know where she'll be, where I know I'll come home to her and where I know I can fuck her anytime I want. I don't want to have to go to another house to do it. It's pointless. You're stayin' here with me."

"But what happens if I don't like your house when I can see?"

"Fuck me," Blue sighed.

I was being silly. I knew I already liked his house; it was all Blue—wooden floor, rugs, a large kitchen, four bedrooms, two bathrooms and two living areas. It was big, and I just knew it would be beautiful, because it belonged to my man.

However, I was surprised and put on the spot. I didn't know he wanted me to live with him permanently. I didn't know he was ready for that step. I wasn't even sure *I* was ready for that step. What I did know was that I never wanted another man; Blue was it for me. I just wanted to give him the opportunity to have his space, and looking for a place was me giving him that.

But he didn't want it.

I smiled.

"She gets it," Blue uttered with a grin in his voice.

"Now it's definitely time for us to go," Zara said, who also had a grin in her voice. "Clary, we'll talk soon. Take care, hun."

"You, too. Bye, Ivy, thank you both for coming. Sorry it seems I've wasted your time."

"No time wasted at all, sweetie," Ivy said. "Later, Blue."

"Yep, see ya."

Are you going to walk them out?" I asked Blue as I heard their footsteps leaving the kitchen.

"Nope."

"Blue, it's the nice thing to do."

"I ain't nice. Not when my woman just agreed to move in with me permanently and I want to fuck her for it."

"Oh, um, okay then." I smirked and stood when I heard the front door open and close quickly. "But I didn't really agree. I was more forced into it."

"Either way, I'm fuckin' happy. Get naked, baby."

"What? Here? Now?"

"Shit yes, I wanna take you over the table, so I can remember it every time I sit at it."

"It's a bit unhygienic."

"Sugar, you can clean it later. If you're not naked in five seconds, I'll take you to the front porch and fuck you over that for everyone to see."

Scoffing, I said, "Give me ten at least. These boots are

buggers to get off." Sitting back down, I started with my left boot and then the right. I could sense Blue coming closer, and I bit my bottom lip from grinning like a loon. He was stalking me and I liked it. After my boots and socks were off, I reached for the bottom of my tee and started to take it off.

A hand landed on my arm. "Slowly," Blue said, his voice dripping with heat.

I crossed my hands over in front of me and gripped my tee again. I slowly slid it up my body and dropped it to the floor. Just to tease, I placed my hands on my breasts, over my bra, and rubbed them, letting a moan fall from my lips.

"That's it, baby," Blue encouraged.

Reaching around to my back, I unhooked my bra and withdrew it from my body, my small handfuls of breasts bouncing slightly. My hands covered them again and I rubbed them around then tweaked my nipples. A shudder ran through my body. I liked that Blue was watching me silently.

Though, he wasn't silent for long. "Take off your jeans, sugar, and sit on the table," he told me.

Standing, I undid my jeans, slid them down my legs, and bent over with my bottom high in the air. He hissed and slapped my arse, making me gasp. When I stood, I flicked them off my feet, turned and sat on the cold, wooden table.

"Spread your legs, Clary. Bare yourself to me." Once I did, Blue groaned and uttered, "Such a beautiful pussy."

Leaning back on the table, resting one hand behind me for support, I then ran my other hand down my other breast, down my stomach, and over my mound.

I heard a zipper sliding undone and clothing being removed, but still, Blue stood away from me.

"I'm gonna palm my dick, baby, as you play with yourself. I wanna see you finger-fuck your sweet pussy."

"Yes," I moaned and rubbed two fingers over my pussy lips; I was already slick with need. I parted them and pinched my clit. "Oh, God," I cried out.

Releasing my clit, I moved my fingers down and slid them straight inside me. I was so wet and aroused I knew it wouldn't take me long to come. Spreading my legs farther apart, I pumped my own fingers in and out of myself.

Stroking sounds met my ears; Blue was indeed masturbating as well. I just wished I could see it. Though, hearing it and listening to his ragged breath was just as amazing.

"Christ, you look gorgeous, Clary."

"Blue, oh, yes. Blue. Babe, I'm gonna come."

"Do it," he growled. "Come all over your fingers. I want to see." I heard him step closer, his hand going to my thigh where he massaged, and just his touch sent me over the edge.

I cried out his name as my pussy spasmed around my

fingers and more of my juices slipped out of me. Blue quickly grabbed my hand, pulling my fingers out of me, only to replace them with his cock. He surged forward and I screamed. "Fuck," he groaned as he plunged back and forth inside me. "You're still comin'. Hell, fuck, baby, you're so tight." He took hold of my arms and brought me up, where he wrapped his arms around my waist so he could attack my mouth with a fierce kiss, all while he fucked me hard and fast.

We broke apart to catch our breath, and just when I went to kiss him again, he groaned, "I'm coming, Christ." He thrust into me three more times and let out a grunted moan, resting his forehead against my chest, and there against me, he said, "Glad we can come to an understanding about you moving in."

I burst out laughing.

CHAPTER TWENTY-ONE

BLUE

*P*acing the floor was all I could do. My body and mind felt wired. I needed something to keep me calm, but that something was my woman, and at that moment, she was why I was wired.

"Brother, she'll be fine," Talon said from where he sat with his wife. I looked over at him and grunted; he smiled. "It's a fuckin' day procedure; they said it's an easy operation. Now stop bloody worrying."

Glaring, I turned on my heels and paced once again. He laughed, and I heard Wildcat's little giggle.

It was easy for him to say; it wasn't his woman in there having some shit done to her eyes. What would happen if they stuffed up the op? What about if they slipped the fuck up and injured her eyes forever? She'd been so excited, so thrilled for the day to come, and just the thought of how her face lit up every time she talked about being able to see again was breath-fuckin'-taking.

Dammit, they had better not fuck anything up, or I'd be killing the lot of them.

The front doors opened, and in came a running Julian.

"I'm here. I'm here. Now, where is my buttercup? Is she okay? Have they finished yet? Oh, God, they better do a good job." He stopped in front of us with his hand on his chest, breathing deeply. Mattie sailed into the room behind him with an eye roll.

"I'm sure she'll be fine. They're doing the best job they can," Mattie said, slipping in behind Julian to rub his back.

"The best they can do? That's not enough, not for my Clary. They need to go beyond that. They need to—"

"Miss James' family?" the doctor called.

I turned and marched toward him. His eyes widened for some goddamn reason. "Yeah?" I asked gruffly. He had better give me the right goddamn words.

"Uh, um. Miss James is in recovery. You can go in and see her, but uh… only one at a time."

"How did it go?" Talon asked behind me.

My fist clenched at my sides. I felt Wildcat step close and hold my arm.

"Everything went exceptional." He smiled hesitantly.

"Thank fuck," I breathed. My head hung low, and I closed my eyes, the tension instantly leaving my body.

"Get in there, brother. I'll hold back Julian as much as I can," Talon said.

I looked up then and said to the doctor, who was waiting to guide us into the recovery room, "Two people will be goin' in. Two people who mean a heap to her."

The doctor nodded slowly.

"Julian," I barked, looking over my shoulder at him.

Fuck. He was crying already.

Then, all of a sudden, he stood straight and reined his emotions in. He wiped his eyes and nodded to me.

Maybe there was hope for the guy after all.

"Let's go, sunshine in the skies."

Christ.

Or maybe there wasn't.

CLARINDA

ONE WEEK LATER

Blue had babied me for the week after my operation, and it was sort of driving me crazy, even though it was as sweet as anything, as well. When the hospital released me, he brought me to his house—or rather *our* house—he placed me in bed, made sure the patches over my eyes were secure and then went out to the kitchen to cook me up something nice. Since then, he hadn't left my side... well, except when Julian was there doing just the same as Blue, babying me. They both helped me dress, eat and bathe. Blue even tried to brush my teeth for me on the first night, until I snapped at him that I was more than capable of brushing my own goddamn teeth. When he silently left the bathroom after telling me to call when I needed help, I felt guilty.

And even though I was tired as hell, I made it up to him later with a BJ. That was after I fought him to let me do it.

"Blue, it's a blow job. I'm sure I can handle having my mouth on your dick without straining my eyes."

"Baby, I ain't taking the risk."

"Blue, if you don't let me suck your cock, we are going to have huge problems," I huffed and slumped on my back in the bed.

"Sugar, are you fuckin' serious right now? You're going to crack-it because I won't let you suck my dick?"

"Yes," I stated and crossed my arms over my chest.

"Jesus Christ. Next, you'll argue with me about the fact we aren't having sex until you're in the clear. Fine, suck my cock, but I'm fuckin' standing by the no sex until you're all good."

I smiled to myself. No, that argument didn't come about until the next night.

Even though my eyes were patched up and a little tender, I still felt fine. Since I felt fine, *and* because I was in a house with my man, of course I wanted to play.

Friday, the next day, was my next appointment, where the doctor would take off my patches. I was worried I was going to be just as I was.

However, I knew that wasn't going to be the case when I woke up that morning.

I must have slept roughly because when I awoke, I felt no pull of tape over my eyes. Straight away they fluttered opened on their own accord because nothing was against them to stop it from happening. And at first, everything was blurred, until I blinked a few times, and suddenly, it cleared.

Sitting up quickly, I gasped. Tears filled my eyes, and my hand flew to cover my mouth as a sob broke out of me.

"Sugar, are you okay?" Blue asked tiredly, but soon, he was sitting up next to me, saying in a panicked voice, "Clary?"

"Blue…" I didn't have the right words. I wanted to cry in utter bliss because I could see and it was beautiful. The room was light from the blinds being open. I was sitting in Blue's king-sized bed, looking out and around at the soft grey-coloured walls. The floor had scattered clothing, but it made me smile. Blue was obviously one who didn't like to pick up after himself.

"Clary, baby, you're worrying me. Fuck, where are

your patches? Shit." He twisted and turned to search for them in the bed. I looked over at him and saw for the first time, his masculine, tattooed back and shoulders as he shifted about in the bed; his muscles worked overtime as he searched. A tattoo of the word *Hawks* was written across his left side, and on the right side was the word *Forever*. His back also contained some scrollwork at the top; it ran over his shoulder and halfway down his strong arms. Blinking back tears, I reached out and gently traced some lines.

He stiffened, and as he slowly turned, my fingers followed around to the top of his chest, where I read another tattoo which said *No Regrets*.

As I traced those lines of wording, I bit my bottom lip to stop the sob wanting release, but still, it was forceful, wanting to come out, and it eventually broke through. Tears fell down my cheeks as I looked up at my man for the first time.

I gasped, my hand going to my throat. He was more handsome than I had ever pictured. He explained once that he had blond hair, but he didn't tell me how sexy and unruly it was. He'd also said his eyes were blue, but he didn't tell me in detail how they were light blue around the pupil and then surrounding the lighter colour was a darker shade of blue. They were heart-stopping.

"Baby—" he started gently.

Until I interrupted, "Y-you... oh, Blue. You're the sexiest man I have ever seen," I uttered with a sob.

"Fuck, shit, damn, baby." He pulled me into his arms and onto his lap, and as he held me tightly against him, he said, "I'm nothing compared to your beauty, Clarinda James. Just looking at your red hair gets me hard; just seeing your body makes me ache and want to be buried inside you. You're a breathtaking beauty, baby, and I fuckin' cherish each day I have with you, sugar because I have never had the love in me that I have for you."

"B-Blue." I wound my arms around his neck and kissed his collarbone as I whispered, "I love you more than anything in my life. You're my world."

The world suddenly shone.

My world was brought back to life, not only because I could see, but because I was in the arms of the man I loved with every fibre of myself.

Pulling back, I reached up for his cheek and gently ran my fingers over it.

"Make love to me?" I uttered.

"Fuck, yes," he growled. I was on my back in seconds and Blue was over me, gazing down at me. "Baby, as soon as we're done we'll be putting your patches back on."

"What? No, I don't—"

"Clary, it's a day too early. We're goin' to the doctor tomorrow. I don't want anything jeopardising your recovery. I'm willing to do *this*, but I want them back on after."

How could I say no to that?

My man was worried about me, and even though

there was only *one* day to go, I was willing to live in the darkness until then, because since Blue he'd shown me more light, more beauty than I had ever seen or felt in a long time.

So, I was willing to give that to my man.

I grinned up at him. "For you, babe, I'll do that. But you had better make it good for me now."

He chuckled deep. "Hell, I'll make it better than good, sugar. I'll blow your mind."

"Talk's cheap, Blue. Show me."

And he proceeded to do just that.

CHAPTER TWENTY-TWO

ONE MONTH LATER

CLARINDA

*J*t may have taken us a month of settling in, a
month of learning and a month of enjoying
each other, but since that month was over, it was finally
the day.

I was to meet Blue's mother and brother.

Blue had come to me two weeks earlier, while I was
sitting in his large spa bath in the main bathroom. We'd
just eaten dinner, which I cooked and was proud I didn't
poison anyone with, and I decided to relax while Blue

called his mother. So when he came in with a smile on his face, I knew something was happening.

He walked over and sat on the edge. "Clary."

My heart started to beat faster. "Yes?" I asked, drawing out the word.

"I was talking to Mum and Jason."

"Yes?"

"They want to meet you."

My eyes widened and I gasped. Meet his family? Me... to meet his family.

He laughed. "Don't look so scared, baby. You'll be fine."

Fine, I was not. I was oh-so nervous.

What would happen if she didn't like me?

What would happen if his brother thought I wasn't right for Blue?

Oh, God, even his mother—she could tell Blue she didn't like me, and then Blue would listen. I knew how much he cared for his mother. He'd told me all about the problems in their family life, how he'd supported them all, how he cared for them. My heart had ached for his mother, for his brother, and for Blue. All those thoughts ran through my mind on the drive to Caroline Springs.

"Sugar, stop stressin'. We're here anyway." We pulled Blue's truck up in front of a large brick home. I had wanted to take the Harley, but Blue said there was a chance of rain later that day and he didn't want to risk anything. I was disappointed because I couldn't get enough of being on the Harley. Flying through the streets or open road feeling free and fantastic, especially since I got to hold Blue close to me. I enjoyed every moment, and we'd had a lot of those in the past month because Blue never got sick of showing me places or things I'd missed out on in the five years I couldn't see.

Waking every morning was a joy because most times I forgot I would be able to see. When I opened my eyes and everything was in a clear, perfect-coloured picture, a warmth filled the pit of my stomach.

What I loved the most, though, was just sitting in the living room with Blue, watching him while he watched TV, or talking with him and watching his expressions.

However, most of all was when we were in bed together making love.

Just that morning, I awoke with Blue under the sheets and between my legs. I had slept so soundly I hadn't even felt him move my limbs around. But what I could feel happening down below made it that much more special to wake up to. Blue had two fingers inside me, gently driving me insane as he pushed and withdrew them while he sucked on my clit. I flipped the sheet back and looked down, and his heated, gorgeous eyes smiled up at me, crinkling at the corners. With one hard suck, I threw my head back and came hard on his fingers. After I caught my breath, I looked back down to Blue, who was still between my legs, grinning up at me.

"I fuckin' love how you come apart, baby. It's a sight

everyone should see, but no one else ever fuckin' will. Best part is I get to keep it all for myself."

Laughter burst out of me. "You're crazy."

"Yeah, but I'm your kinda crazy."

"That you are," I said. He climbed up and hovered over me. Then Blue pushed his hardness against my mound. "Why, Blue, are you happy to see me?"

"I think it's be more about that you're happy to *see me*."

Giggling, I said, "That I am, and I'll show you how happy it makes me." Slipping my hand between us, I gripped his erect cock and glided my hand up and down it.

"Fuck," he groaned and pumped more eagerly into my hand. Watching lust shine in his eyes as he looked between us and witnessed my hand jacking him off was glorious. The muscles of his arms as he held himself above me tightened, his stomach trembled, and something I would never get tired of tracing and looking at was the V which pointed down to the part of him I was currently playing with.

"Jesus, baby. You keep doing that, and I'll end up coming all over you."

"That's the plan," I whispered and blushed.

"You wanna watch me come on you, sugar?"

"Oh, yes."

"Christ, that's fuckin' hot, baby," he moaned as he pumped faster into my hand. "Shit, Clary, I'm gonna shoot my load all over you."

Hell, I wanted that. I had never in my life seen a man come, never watched it fly out of a man's cock, and I wanted it so much from Blue.

"Ahh, you ready, baby?"

"Yes," I uttered.

"Fuck, look down; here it comes." As he thrust his cock into my hand, white fluid squirted out and onto my naked stomach. He kept thrusting, and more came out as he grunted with deep satisfaction. Once he slowed, I looked up at him and smiled. "Jesus Christ, woman. I fuckin' love the look of awe on your face right now. Had you never seen a guy come before? From porn or anything?" he asked as he pried my hand away from his cock and chuckled.

"No. Remember, your woman has only ever been with one other, and I've never thought about watching any porn. My friends back then weren't into it. Which is why watching you was awesome. Can we do it again?"

He snorted. "Yeah, give me a second."

"Sugar, what are you thinkin' so hard about? Come on, get on out so we can head in."

I blushed. Those naughty thoughts shouldn't have even crossed my mind while sitting out front of his mother's house.

"Now I want to know what you were thinking about

227

to cause you to turn bright red, like your fuckin' amazing hair," Blue teased. He took hold of my hand. "You gonna tell me, baby?"

"Um… no. Now isn't really the time."

"Clary, now is definitely the fuckin' time."

I rolled my eyes at him and looked at our joined hands. I knew he wouldn't let up so we could get into his mum's house and get the frightful day out of the way, so I mumbled, "You. I was thinking of you and what we did this morning."

He placed a hand under my chin, tipping my head up and sideways so I was looking at him. His warm, lust-filled eyes stared back. "You really liked that, yeah?"

"Yes,"

"Good, 'cause it's gonna happen again and again. We'll learn about each other, test each other out to see what we like. Hell, we'll even watch porn together, and I can't fuckin' wait."

Grinning, I said, "Me neither."

"Now, let's go see my family." He gestured with his chin to the house again, and I turned to look and spotted a lovely looking older woman dressed in a spring, flowery dress, smiling from the front porch.

I jumped when I heard Blue's door slam. He was around to my side seconds later and opening my door. With his hand outstretched to me, I paused for a moment.

Really, what I wanted to do was crawl in the backseat and pretend I wasn't there.

It was a big step for me, though I'd had many big steps over a short amount of time. Never in the five years I was blind had I thought I'd be able to see again, never had I thought I'd meet the man who was made just for me and never had I thought I would be living with that man and meeting his family.

I was a little overwhelmed.

"Sugar, come on. It's gonna be okay."

Looking up at my man, I believed him. His warm eyes told me to trust him, and I did. So I smiled, took his hand and climbed out of the car.

After he shut my door and locked it, he removed his hand from mine, and I think I whimpered. He quickly placed his arm around my waist so he could steer me up the front path to his waiting mother.

"Hey, Mum," Blue said, smiling big as we stood just below the porch. "This is Clarinda James. She's really nervous and thinks you're gonna hate her."

"Blue," I snapped and slapped him in the stomach.

Mrs Skies laughed loudly and then said, "Oh, honey, there is no way I could hate you. In fact, I already love you for making my boy here so happy."

Blushing, I uttered, "Um, thank you."

"Are they here? Is she pretty?" we heard yelled from the house.

Blue laughed and explained, "That'll be my brother Jason. Sometimes he doesn't have a filter."

"I guess he takes after his older brother then." I smirked.

Mrs Skies giggled. "She knows you well, Blue," she said as a younger version of Blue came running out onto the front porch to stand behind his mum.

His smile was gorgeous and infectious. I couldn't help but smile back and give him a little finger wave.

"Adele, they're here, and she's *real* pretty!" he yelled back into the house. When he turned back to us, he added, "You're too pretty for my brother."

"Hey, kid," Blue mock-growled.

"What? It's the truth." He grinned. "Come on in and meet Adele. She's really funny and swears a lot." Jason ended up reaching around his mum and out to me. Taking my hand in his, he pulled me toward the front door.

I glanced over my shoulder to smile and shrug at Blue. He beamed, and then stepped up to his mum to place his arm around her shoulders and lead her in after us. "Oh, and you'll get to meet Memphis. He was Blue's friend, but he's Mum's boyfriend now." He paused to lean in and whisper while walking me down the long hallway. "At first, I thought he was Blue's boyfriend, but Blue told me he wasn't gay, and now you're here, so I guess he was telling the truth." Laughter bubbled up and out of me as I heard a deep groan behind us. I just knew I was going to love Jason.

The day was perfect. Jason had been right about Adele; she was very funny, teasing Blue a lot and telling me some stories about his past. The best one yet was when he'd come home one night for a visit, only to walk back out the door with some mates, and then come back again totally drunk, where he proceeded to propose to Adele. When she knocked back the offer, she swore he was going to cry. That was when Blue yelled, "I had something in my fuckin' eye!" We all burst out laughing as Blue sat there grumbling, though he didn't look too upset at all.

Memphis was quiet. I wasn't too sure of him... until I saw the looks he sent Blue's mum. He totally adored her. So if Blue and his family liked him, I guessed I could warm to the guy, as well.

After lunch, I was surprised when Blue suggested a walk. We ended up walking to an ice cream shop, where Blue and Jason then tried to outdo each other to see who could eat their ice cream first. Again, we all finished in a fit of laughter when they both got brain freeze.

As we were leaving, Mrs Skies pulled me aside to say goodbye. I could hear Blue and Jason talking quietly in the hall while I stood in the living room.

She asked me to sit next to her on the couch, and when I did, she took my hand in both of hers. "I loved today, Clary." She smiled, using the nickname Blue and my friends called me. "I especially loved today, because I got to see my boy shine. I have never seen him so relaxed, so content in life and I have to say you brought him that. So I wanted to pull you aside to say thank you. Thank you for taking care of my son, and thank you for loving him. He deserves so much, and I believe he will find all the happiness in life with you by his side."

Tears pooled in my eyes. I didn't know what to say, because she was wrong. It was the other way around; Blue had been the one to bring happiness and love into *my* life.

Though, to give her what she wanted, I said, "I wouldn't have it any other way. He means the world to me, and I am grateful every day to have found him."

"You ready, baby?" Blue asked from the doorway.

Had he heard what I just said?

From his soft eyes, small, sensual smile and the fast rise and fall of his chest, I could say he had and he liked what he heard.

On the way home, he showed me exactly how he liked what I said to his mum. He pulled his truck to the side of the road, and before I knew what was going on, he undid both our seatbelts, pushed his seat back as far it would go, and then I was in his lap, straddling his waist.

"Best fuckin' day of my life," he growled and cupped my face in his hands. "Shit, no, I take that back. Best day was when I saw you, then when I spoke to you, and then when you told me you wanted to suck my cock for the first time and then… when you told me you loved me. So this day is up there with all of them. Hell, I know we'll have a lot more, but what you said to my mum, what you shared was fuckin' beautiful. I knew she'd been worried about me, and I knew if she saw me with you she would settle, and she did, but she didn't settle totally until you shared those words with her. I saw it, in her body and face. You made her day, and in return, you made mine." His grin was wicked. "So now, I'm gonna make it one of your best days."

Smiling, I shook my head. "Too late, babe. It already is, I love your family, Blue."

"And they love you. Still, I'm having you here right now to show you what you mean to me. To show you how much I love you."

I squirmed on his lap, rubbing my centre over his erection. "Well, you better get started."

He chuckled. "Gladly."

CHAPTER TWENTY-THREE

TWO MONTHS LATER

BLUE

*S*itting at the bar alone, having a refreshing beer while I waited for Clary to finish her hair appointment, my thoughts drifted to the talk I had with Talon the day before when we were in the garage fixing up some shit-heap of a car.

"How's things going with your woman?" he'd asked.

He didn't miss the smile on my face from just the mention of her. "Yeah, good, brother. Never thought I'd find a woman to breathe easy with, but I have, and there ain't no way I'm giving that up."

"Did you tell her about the court case?"

I sighed. "Hell, yes. I ain't hiding anything again. I told her the day it happened, two motherfuckin' days ago. When she found out her sister and Henry both got ten years for kidnapping and attempted murder, she sat there stunned for a moment, and then shrugged and said, 'Okay.' Not sure if she's really taken that in."

"I was talkin' to Zara last night. She has, my man. Zara had asked her about it yesterday at their pow-wow, and she said Clary didn't really care, because that part of her life was over and she wasn't willing to deal with it again, not now she has a new happy life... with her man." He smirked.

I chuckled and said, "Good to fuckin' know."

He laughed. "No worries." He leaned over the engine again, tightening up some bolts. "Spoke with Memphis last night, too."

"How's he handling it all?" I asked.

"Yeah, damn good."

"Told you he'd be right for the prez job there."

"All right, arsehole, you can be right sometimes. How you dealin' with him and your ma?"

"Still freaks me the fuck out, but he's been good for her. Actually, I was thinkin' of taking Clary there again. Mum loved her."

"I can see why; she's good for you."

Grinning, I said, "Yeah, I know."

We went back to work for a few moments, and then Talon shocked the shit outta me and asked, "When you puttin' a ring on her finger, so all fellas know she's yours?"

Nearly choking on my saliva, I said, "Ah, soon, I guess."

"Brother, I've fuckin' seen the way the single brothers around here keep an eye on her. They're waitin' for you to stuff up."

"Won't fuckin' happen," I growled.

Talon chuckled. "Dude, I'm bloody joking. All the brothers know you'd slit their throats if they tried anything."

"Yeah, thanks, dick, for gettin' me worked up."

But he had been right. I'd been thinkin' more and more about puttin' a ring on my old lady's finger. That time was certainly coming soon.

"Yo, another beer," I called to the bartender. He sent me a chin lift as my phone started to ring in my pocket. I pulled it free with a smile on my face, thinking it would be my woman.

I was so fucking wrong.

The number was private, so I answered with, "Yeah?"

"Blue," a deep voice drew out my name.

"Who's this?" I asked with an annoyed tone.

"I'm hurt you don't remember my voice," he said with a smile. "Especially after you beat the shit out of me." My body jacked up straight. "Oh, well, I guess you'll remember me when I tell you I have your idiot brother."

Fuck!

"Motley," I barked.

"Oh, Blue, I'm touched. You *do* remember me."

"What the fuck are you doin' with my brother?"

He chuckled. "I've learned so many things these past weeks, my brother."

"I'm no brother of yours. Tell me what you want, and if you harm *my* brother, you will fuckin' pay with your life."

"Now isn't the time for threats, Blue. Not when I have the upper-hand."

"What. Do. You. Fuckin'. Want?" I banged my fist on the table. Hell, if he'd laid a finger on Jason, I would make his death slow and painful.

"I have a brother on the inside, and he was talking to another friend of yours. Henry."

Motherfucking Christ.

"I want your woman in exchange for your brother."

Closing my eyes, I slumped in my seat.

My woman or my brother.

Jesus.

"No," I uttered.

A gun fired in the background, and I heard Jason scream my name.

"Wait, you fuckin' wait, you motherfucker!" I yelled into the phone as I strode from the bar. "I goddamn meant no to both of them. You can have me instead."

He laughed. "Well, it was lucky my friend missed his shot and your brother is still breathing. However, I don't want you. I can make a hell of a lot of money off your woman, and while I'm at it, I'd have some fun along the way."

"I have more money than she does. If you want money, I'll fuckin' sign it all over to you, and then you can do with me what you want if I witness my brother walkin' free from you."

"You're not really my type… but, I do love a bit of payback. You have a deal, Blue. Come set your brother free and sign over your money."

"You'll leave Clary out of this?"

He laughed. "Pinkie swear, brother."

Fuck.

He was lying. I had to get eyes on my woman and now.

"Where do I go?"

He said an address in Caroline Springs and then added, "But I wouldn't go and tell anyone. We'll be moving as soon as you hit here. And if you plan anything to happen before you get here, expect your brother to be dead."

"I need to confirm it *is* him you have."

The phone got shuffled around, and then my heart convulsed when I heard, "Blue?" *Christ, Jesus Christ, he sounds scared.* "Don't you come, Blue. You stay safe and keep Clary out of this. I'm fine, Blue. I'm a man. I can take this."

Oh, fuck.

Hell no. No, no, no.

"Jason, stay strong for me, little brother."

"Blue—"

"No, buddy. I know you're a man, but you need to be a man who will take care of Mum. You stay strong. You hear me? I'll be there soon."

"Okay, Blue. I can do that for you."

Shit, shit, shit.

He was lying, as well.

"Jason," I growled.

"Bye, Blue. I love you."

"Jason, don't—" The line went dead. The fucking line went dead and my heart went there with it.

FUCK.

My hand itched to hit somethin', to throw my goddamn phone down, but I did nothing because I had shit to do.

Pressing a button, I put the phone to my ear once again.

"Speak," Talon barked.

"Motley has my brother. I'm going to him now, hopefully before Jason does something stupid. He wants money. He asked to swap Clary for Jason. Henry told him she had money. I told him no that I had more money. He agreed to take me so that I can sign it all over to him, and he can have his payback from when I beat the fuck outta him. I need eyes on Clary right now. I don't trust the fucker. Ring Memphis; he'll need to be there for Mum." I paused for a second. "Brother, if I don't... you know what to do. Take care of them all."

"Blue, brother, we can fuckin' deal with this dick. He

can't do this. We need to make plans. Come to the goddamn compound and we'll sort something out."

Looking up at the sky, I said, "No. I'm going in alone," and then hung up. It started ringing straight away. I hit the end button and rang the next person before I hit the road.

"Hey, babe. I'm nearly done, probably about another twenty. You're going to love it, Blue, and when you tell me that, I expect you to show me how much you love it," my woman said with a smile in her voice.

My throat got thick. Shit, I was going to miss her.

Fuck. I was going to miss my life with her.

For a selfish reason alone, I wished I had put that ring on her finger sooner.

"Clary," I whispered.

"Blue, what's wrong?"

Christ, she knew something was up from just my voice.

"Baby, you know I love you, yeah?"

"Blue," her voice caught, "you're scaring me, handsome." I heard her shoo someone away.

Taking a breath, I said, "I have to head out of town for a couple of days. Family shit. Not that you aren't family, but it's somethin' only I can deal with it." Another breath. "Clary, you are everything to me. You remember that always."

"Blue, please, whatever it is, we can do it together. Please, babe… please don't leave without me."

"I love you, baby."

"Blue, please," she whispered into the phone.

Hell, she was crying now.

"Clary, I love you."

"Blue—"

"Sugar, *please*. I love you."

"I love you, too, Blue Skies. I love you more than my own life. But I want you to wait for me. I'm leaving now. I'll come with you. I need to be with you, Blue."

"I'll always be with you, Clarinda," I uttered and then hung up the phone.

CLARINDA

No, please no. I ran from the hairdresser's with tears streaming down my face. Something was wrong, so very, very wrong, and I had to get to my man. I had to help him.

In the car, I took a breath but realised I was wasting time. I just hoped I wasn't too late.

God, please don't let me be too late.

As I sped through the streets, I picked up my phone and pressed the call button. "Hey, hun. How's the hair look?" Zara asked.

"Something is wrong, Zara. Blue called while I was at the hairdresser, telling me how much he loved me and I meant everything to him. Zara... honey, he sounded so deflated. Something's wrong. I need to know what. He said he's going out of town for a few days. I asked him to wait for me. I'm on my way to our house now." A pause, and then, "Zara, I'm scared. I know it has something to do with his family, and I'm scared that if he doesn't wait for me, he'll go on his own and I won't see him again." A sob tore through. "I don't know what to do. I can't lose him. I can't live without him, but I just know he's gone and thrown the gauntlet down on whatever the situation is."

"Clary, listen to me. I'll get the girls. We'll meet you at your house and if we can't get answers, I know who will give them to us."

"Okay, okay, thank you," I uttered and threw the phone to the passenger seat. Five blocks from home and I had never driven Blue's truck so fast before. I pulled into the driveway and got out, leaving the door open. I ran for the house and twisted the handle. It was locked.

No. Fuck, no.

My head leaned against it.

It was locked.

It meant I was too late. Either he had come and gone already, or he hadn't even been there in the first place. Though I needed to confirm, so I unlocked the door with shaking hands and pushed it open. The house smelled of Blue, but then again, it always did. I frantically ran from one room to another, calling his name.

He didn't answer.

"Clary?" Zara yelled from the front door. I ran back down the long hall and into the living room, where Zara, Deanna, and Ivy were walking in.

"He's not here," I cried. "He's not here. I just know he's out doing something silly, something dangerous. What do I do? I don't know what to do." I went to my knees on the hard wooden floor.

Deanna was at my side first. "We'll find the dick, and we'll figure out what's going on. Then once we find him, I'm going to rip his dick off and give it to Julian for Christmas." She knelt down next to me, rubbing my back. "Come on, get up. We know where to go to get the right answers."

CHAPTER TWENTY-FOUR

BLUE

I pulled my Harley into the drive of some old, ratty joint. The weatherboard home had seen better days. Climbing off quickly, I made my way to the front door, but then the noise of the garage door being opened caught my attention. I turned my head toward it and found Motley walking out. He stopped to the side of it and smiled at me. A car started up and drove forward, a white van with some plumbing signage on the side of it.

Motley gestured with his head to the van. "Get in the back."

"Where's my brother?" I growled.

"We're taking you to him. Get the fuck in the back, Blue." He turned to some other guys I didn't know and ordered, "Load up his bike in the other van. I want no trace he was here."

Striding to the van with my fists clenched at my sides and a foul look in my eyes had Motley taking a step back. I smiled, letting him know I saw it, and then I walked to the side of the van and climbed in the back.

I needed to get to my brother.

As soon as Motley was in the passenger side, we took off. I was passed a blindfold and told to put it on. I knew they were waiting for me to fight back, for me to argue, but there was no way in Hell I would do anything until my brother was safe.

We drove for what seemed like almost an hour. The van stopped, my side door came open and I was roughly pulled from it. The blindfold was taken from my eyes and I blinked up at the sudden glare of the sun.

I searched my surroundings and saw we were in bushland somewhere, and they were forcing me toward an old, beat-up farmhouse. The front door opened, and another guy stepped out and held it open as Motley shoved me over the threshold.

I scoffed. "What, you're not gonna carry me over? It is our first night together."

"Shut the fuck up!" Motley yelled and pushed me through another doorway to the right.

That was when I saw my brother.

And I did not like what I saw.

He was bloodied and bruised, sitting on a mattress in the corner of the room.

A roar filled my lungs and tumbled over. They hurt my brother. They made my brother bleed.

They would fucking pay.

Ripping my arms from Motley, I tackled the closest guy, and sitting on him, I landed punch after punch to his face. When I knew he wouldn't move again, I was on my feet, ready to take on the next fucker.

"Blue!" Motley screamed.

I turned to look at him, my gaze low, my breath heavy. I wanted more fuckers to pay. I wanted blood on my hands for what they did. I wanted them to drown in so much pain.

Standing straight, I tried to calm myself and let the fight flee my body because Motley had a gun trained on my brother.

"Jason?" I called.

"I'm okay," he whispered and tried to smile, only it wasn't real. He was in pain and was trying not to let me see it.

"You can blame him for this. He tried to escape. We couldn't have that now."

"He was to be unharmed, and he was to go free when I arrived," I snarled.

"Change of plans." Motley grinned, and then all the lights went out for me as something hit me in the back of the head.

I AWOKE TIED to a chair in the middle of the living room. Shaking my head to clear it was a bad fucking idea; the pain throbbed through the back of my skull. Still, I looked over to the side to see Jason lying on a dirtied mattress.

I'd failed to protect him.

I'd failed my brother.

That hurt. It hurt so damn much.

Motley came charging into the room with paper flapping in his hand. He dragged a damaged, old coffee table over in front of me, slammed the papers down and held out a pen. "Sign," he barked.

I laughed. "What, you want me to hold it in my teeth? Won't look fuckin' real then."

"If I untie you, you better sign."

Sighing, I said, "I ain't signing shit until my brother's free." I kicked the table over on its side. Jason jumped from the sound of it clattered to the ground. He sat up and eyed us both as we glared at each other.

"You stupid, motherfucking arsehole. You think you're so good being under Talon? I'll teach you you're nothing. You'll have nothing when I'm done with you," Motley spat as he leaned over me.

Fuck. It killed me Jason would be witness to all this.

To his brother being tortured and beaten.

"You're the only stupid fuck, Motley," I growled. "If I don't get what I want, then you don't either."

Motley laughed. "I'll go after your sweet girl. I saw the both of you walking the street with your mum and brother. Smiling, laughing, being happy. If you don't sign it all over to me, I'll make her pay as well."

"You will not fuckin' touch her," I roared.

"Blue, Blue, just do it. Just sign, Blue, please," my brother pleaded.

"Jason, no."

"He's gonna kill us anyway; at least I'll go with my brother at my side."

Fuck. Shit, shit, shit.

"Jason—"

"Don't let him hurt Clary. She's too good. Don't let him do that to her."

"Christ," I uttered. "I'm sorry, Jason."

"I'm not. I'm not sorry about anything. I'm proud to call you my brother. You came here for me anyway, knowing we wouldn't come out of this. I love you, Blue."

"Goddammit, I love you, too, kid."

"Yeah, yeah, this is really sweet and all, but sign the fucking papers!" Motley yelled.

Looking from Jason, I turned my hard stare to Motley. He would never get what he wanted. I would never let that happen because I knew Talon would keep his word. He would take care of Clary, and he would take care of our mum... until his last breath.

"No," I whispered harshly.

"Blue!" Jason yelled.

"Jason, brother. Don't you see?" I asked, and then as I stared at Motley, I told Jason, "Motley here has already seen it in me that I won't sign anything over. He should have taken the chance with Clary, but he was stupid enough to accept my offer. He'll never get his hands on her. Talon will protect her with his life, and not only her, but he'll take care of Mum too. He made that promise to me before I came... and a brother in arms never goes back on a promise. Do they, Motley?"

Jason actually laughed.

But then, Motley's scream soon filled the room.

Since he knew he was never going to get what he wanted, it was time to move onto the next stage.

And that stage was ending my life.

Only, it'd be with a fight on his hands.

He pulled a gun from behind him and raised it. I stood, taking the chair I was tied to with me and jumped in front of Jason as he fired.

TALON

TWO HOURS EARLIER

The door to my office burst open and then slammed shut after Griz marched in with Stoke, Killer, Pick, Billy, and Dodge. As soon as I got off the fucking phone with Blue, I had called all brothers out to play. Most were out searching for him, and two—Judge and Tank—I'd sent to Vi's office. Not many knew, but I had her guys install trackers on my brothers' bikes, and thank fuck I did. As soon as they found out which way Blue was heading, we were getting on our bikes and riding out.

"Have you rang Memphis?" Killer asked.

"Yeah, brother. He was at the compound, but he's on his way to his woman and informing her that her boys are in deep shit." *Fuck this and the goddamn situation.*

Jesus, Blue had just gotten to a motherfucking happy place, and then another arsehole messed it all up.

They were gonna pay. Pay in blood.

I stood from my chair and swiped everything from my desk onto the floor. "Fuck!" I yelled.

"Talon, why in the fuck did the jackarse not wait for us? Not wait for some type of help?" Griz snapped.

Shaking my head, I said, "I think he was worried he was gonna be too late. He was worried his brother was gonna do somethin' crazy."

"Fuck," Stoke hissed.

"Where's Clary?" Billy asked.

"I've sent brothers out to look for her. I need eyes on

her now. Blue was worried Motley would make a play to get her as well."

"Motherfucker," Pick growled.

My door burst open once again. We all looked over to see Clary with wild eyes, Hell Mouth with determined ones, Ivy with angry ones and my woman's eyes fell on me, and they were pissed.

"Look—" I started.

"I don't want bullshit," Clary said. "My man called me and I could hear something in his voice which has me freaked out. Something is going on with his family, and I need to know what it is, and now, so I can get there and help him."

"Billy, go call Shift, Gun and Watt. Tell them Blue's woman is here and safe," I ordered. Billy gave me a chin lift and left the room. "Clary, it's good you're here. Blue wants you to stay here and safe."

"What's going on?" Clary asked in a quiet voice.

"Not sure if you should know."

"Not sure if I should know? *You're* not sure if *I* should know something which concerns my man? Something which obviously has stirred you all up to have everyone running everywhere. Something which is goddamn dangerous, and something my man has just fucking walked into, and still, you don't think I should know?"

"Jesus, I can see why Blue fell hard for her," Stoke muttered.

"Just tell her," my woman uttered.

"Kitten."

"No, honey. If it were me, I would want to know. If someone didn't tell me, then I would hate that person with a vengeance, because if it were you, Talon, I would be..." She shook her head. "...it wouldn't be good. Please, just tell her."

"Fuck." I sighed. "All right."

CLARINDA

Never have I hated someone so much before. Not even my sister. But right then, I hated the man who took my lifeline from me, who took the man I loved and who took an innocent boy from the safety of his family, just to have payback because he wasn't man enough to run a goddamn bikers' club. Because he was lazy, sleazy and dirty in every way and form.

After Talon and Griz told me all they knew, I was ready to rip shreds through anything and anyone to get to Blue and Jason.

But then, Talon informed me fucking Motley wanted me in replacement for Jason...for money.

Why did it always come down to money?

Blue was smart enough to trade himself for me because if I had found out first, I would have been where

Blue was. I would not have left Jason in the hands of the cruel bastard.

Blue was protecting me once again.

It was time I protected him.

I needed to get him back.

The only funny side to the situation was when Talon and his men tried to stop me from coming to Blue's rescue because that was when Ivy stepped forward before me and let them have it.

She must have read every furious emotion I had upon my face because she relayed everything I wanted to say.

With a hand on my arm, she stepped beyond me, and with a glare in her eyes, she said to Talon, Griz, Stoke, Killer, Pick and Dodge, "Listen here, you bad-arse mofos. We get that you want to go in all gung-ho; it's your biker brother, so of course we understand that. But you need to understand Clary needs to be in on this. It's her man in danger, and I can tell you now if it was any of you, we'd," she gestured to us standing in front of Talon's desk, "be doing the same. You all helped us through our Hell. You sacrificed yourselves *through* our Hell; let it be our turn to help to sacrifice. Now, I'm not saying we're going to go in there without you and be stupid-like. We need guns and other shit, too. But what I'm also saying is you either accept that we *are* coming, not only for you, but for Clary, or else we'll go it alone, and I'm sure you all know that could be just as dangerous. I can promise we'll listen, we'll do as we're told, and we won't be more of a distraction to you to get Blue and Jason out safely. We will be the best team-mates you've ever had. We will listen… okay, I will, and I'm sure Clary and Zara will. Deanna, I'm not so sure about."

"Hey," Deanna snapped and then sighed. "If I'm in on it, I promise I'll be on my best fuckin' behaviour."

"Please," I begged. "Please let us do this, and *now,* so I can get Blue back in one piece." I held back the urge to cry at the thought of Blue being hurt. I held back the sob that wanted to fall out of me. I held it all back because it was what I wanted to do. I needed to be there to help my man.

"Shit, I'm going to regret this." Talon sighed. He turned to Griz and said, "Get a brother at Vi's on the phone. Find out where we're heading so we can roll."

That was when I smiled for the first time since Blue's phone call.

CHAPTER TWENTY-FIVE

CLARINDA

*W*e had a plan, and it was a good one. At least, I hoped it was. We were still trying to figure it out on the way. Vi had told Talon that Blue's Harley stopped at a house in Caroline Springs, but then, after moments, it continued on. Now it was parked in outer Melton. From the Google Maps app, it showed he was in a secluded area surrounded by bushland. The Hawks crew dumped their Harleys to ride in vans. Altogether, there were four vans with around five to ten bikers in each one. I was riding in the back of one with Deanna, Zara, Ivy, Talon, Griz, and Killer. Dodge, Pick, and Stoke were up front.

"We can't just go running in there. We don't know

what type of situation Blue and Jason are in, and we don't know how many men this Motley guy has. If we run in there, we could risk hurting Blue more. I won't have that," I said.

"Awww, listen to you. So glad you jumped right into your bad-arse biker bitch ways." Deanna smiled. "Too bad it was because of something so fucked-up."

Talon, ignoring Deanna, said, "We'll park away and go in on foot. We'll do all the fuckin' recon we need to before anything happens. There is no way I would risk my brother."

"Good, that's good." I nodded.

"Um, I have a plan," Ivy started.

"Cupcake," Killer clipped.

Cupcake?

She rolled her eyes at her man and continued, "We need someone to go in and see what's going on inside, right? Well, I was thinking of strippers."

"I don't think male strippers would be good right now, Chatter," Deanna stated with a snort.

"No, I don't mean male strippers. I mean I was thinking that we," Ivy gestured to us women, "could walk up to the door and pretend we're looking for a place close by, but we got lost, and then we can be all worried because we were going to lose money for being late. They may or may not let us in the house for their own enter-tainment, and if they do, one of us can sneak off to go to the toilet and scope out the place. Then we inform the guys of where and when they can come bursting in to save the day."

Silence filled the van as we all stared at her.

"What?" she asked. "I didn't just come up with it. It's always been a fantasy of mine to pretend to be a stripper and knock on Fox's front door, and then he could have his wicked way with me. But before that, I'd be all shy and give him a lap dance—"

"Ivy," Killer snapped.

"Too much?" she asked, blushing.

He lowered his head and nodded, but everyone could see the smirk on his face. He looked back up and said, "Precious, it's a great fuckin' plan, but I ain't lettin' it happen. No one sees your body but me, and if they even thought of fuckin' touchin' you, I'd have to kill them."

Holy shit. I knew he was serious.

"I'll do it," Deanna said.

"Princess," Griz groaned.

"And me," Zara added.

"Kitten, no fuckin' way."

"Of course I'm doing it," I said.

"That's a hell fuckin' no," Talon growled out. "To you all. Besides, they know what you look like, Clary."

"I think it's goddamn brilliant," Stoke said from up front. "Hell, I know if your women came knockin' on my door, I'd be dragging them in to see the moves they had."

Pick reached over and hit him in the back of the head. "Christ; think, man, think."

"Stoke's right, for once," Dodge said. "It's a good plan, and if it doesn't work, so be it, and they leave. But if it does, then we have eyes on the inside. It's the best way to get Blue out without fuckin' it all up. Besides Clary, the three of them should do it. Better in numbers." He stopped to look in the rear-view mirror. "I know it's all your women, but it'll fuckin' work, and you know this, boss. Let them do it."

"Fuck," Killer hissed.

"Christ," came from Griz.

"I shouldn't have fuckin' brought them," Talon complained.

Stoke cleared his throat. "But you ladies can't go in like that." The women looked at each other and realised he was right; jeans and tees just wouldn't grab a man's attention.

"Does someone have a knife?" I asked.

AFTER I DID a little renovation on their clothes by cutting their jeans into Daisy-Duke shorts and trimming their tees, so they just sat up under their breasts, we pulled to a stop in a picnic area which was close to the house.

We climbed out of the back, and as soon as we did, Talon snarled to his men, "Keep your fuckin' eyes to yourself."

Then Killer added, "Or I'll snap you in two."

Finally, Griz stated, "And if he doesn't, I fuckin' will. Jesus Christ, Stoke that means you, too. Get your goddamn eyes off my woman's arse."

"Okay, guys," I called. "Talon will fill you in." As they huddled around talking through the plan, I met with the ladies at the front of the van. "Thank you for doing this."

"Hell, I love this shit," Deanna laughed.

"I do like seeing Fox all bossy male." Ivy smiled.

"Hun," Zara said, and I looked at her. "You would have done the same for us if it was our men, but it's not only that. Blue and Jason are family to our crazy bunch."

Tears filled my eyes. "I know; it's just…."

"Nothing will happen to him or us, so don't start your shit," Deanna barked.

Snorting, I rolled my eyes at her. "You have your phones?"

They patted their bras and nodded. Each one of them was going in there with their man on the other end of that phone in their bras, so the men could hear everything going on. I stepped up to Zara and pulled the elastic which held up her long, thick dark hair from its hold. It fell around her shoulders. Ivy's hair was already flowing around her shoulders and looking sexy. I then went to Deanna and asked her to turn; she glared at me but did it. I pulled her hair free of her elastic, only to tie it back up, but in pigtails. It made her look so much cuter and approachable… if she got rid of her scowl.

"Are you serious?" she snapped.

"Yes." I grinned. "Griz," I called. He turned, his eyes landing right on Deanna, and then they widened, and he said, "Fuck me."

Deanna laughed and said, "Well, okay then."

The men had a final chat with their women, and after a heated kiss, they sent them on their way.

Talon turned to all of us and said, "Let's head out. Everyone fuckin' quiet." And then we started our walk through the bush.

We were nearing the final destination point when Killer, Griz and Talon's phones vibrated in their pockets. The women took longer to get there because they had to take the long road around in the van when we were cutting through.

Talon handed his phone off to me and said, "You listen. I need my head in the game. Keep me posted."

I nodded and placed his phone up to my ear as we all walked silently through the bush.

On the phone, I heard Zara open the car door. "Why, hello there, handsome," she cooed at someone. "We're a little lost. Could you help us? Barbie, honey, what was that address again?"

"Aww, gee, Honey, I'm not sure. Candy, do you know it?" I heard Deanna ask. Griz grumbled about something to my left, but I ignored him and held the phone tighter to my ear.

Candy who was actually Ivy mentioned an address, and that was when I heard a male say,

"Ladies, I'm sorry to say but that's a house up the road."

"Dang it, we're already late. Now we won't get paid," Zara sulked.

They were all great actresses.

"Don't be upset, pretty lady," a new man's voice said.

"But we needed the money. Candy wanted to get her boob job done, and now she won't have enough money." Deanna sighed, and she sounded absolutely deflated.

"You don't look like you need a boob job, sweetie."

"Oh, thank you. That is so sweet of you, but my man just isn't giving me enough attention, and he said he won't until I have my boobs done."

"Stupid motherfucking plan," Killer hissed.

"D-do you think... no, that's rude of me," Zara said.

"What ya gonna ask there, beautiful? Come on, don't be shy."

"Well... I... um, I kind of hoped you guys would care for a private show, and maybe...oh, gosh, maybe you could pay us, so Candy can get her boobs?"

"O-M-G, Honey, that's a great idea! Then I won't have to disappoint my man. Oh, oh, will you guys do that? Will you help us out?"

The men chuckled, and one said, "I'm sure we can come up with something."

"Yeah, we'd hate for you to be upset. Come on inside."

Footsteps sounded on a gravel path, and then it changed, got louder. They must have been on the front porch. A door opened, and the men beckoned them inside. The ladies giggled with fake glee and commented on the house as one guy called for someone.

I gasped and looked to Griz. Did someone just call for Motley? Griz nodded to my silent question.

"What's this we have here?" Motley asked.

"Some strippers were s'posed to be at the house down the road, but they took a wrong turn, and now they're late and won't get paid. They needed some money, boss."

Motley chuckled. "And what are they willing to do for that money?"

"Anything. I'm really good at lap dancing, and if you had a pole, Candy loves to swing around one. And Honey can turn a man on with just a wiggle of her hips," Deanna said.

"Show us."

"D-do you have some music?" Ivy asked. She was starting to sound nervous.

Looking over to Killer, I knew from his drawn brows and clenched jaw he was thinking the same thing, and he was worried.

"I'm sure we can get some. Barry, find a fuckin' radio or some shit. It's about time we had some fun, 'til the wanker wakes up."

"Oh, is someone asleep? Maybe we shouldn't disturb him. I'd hate to make anyone cranky," Zara said.

"Sweetheart, you couldn't make anyone cranky with your face like an angel. The other guy will be in no shape to even care. How about you come here to Daddy? I'll take care of you."

"But I wanted to show you my moves first. Please, I'm really good."

"Barry, hurry the fuck up!" Motley yelled.

"I'm here, got one. Let's get this party started."

"One second. Honey, didn't you say you had to use the loo in the car?" Ivy asked with confidence back in her voice.

"Look at that; you're making her blush. Sweetheart, do you need to go?"

"Yes," Zara uttered.

"Just down the hall, last door on the right."

"Thank you, handsome, and then I'll come back and show you my moves."

"I look forward to it." I heard a slap and Zara squealed. He must have smacked her butt.

Thank God Talon wasn't listening; instead, he was hidden behind some trees, scoping out the house.

"Okay, I'm in the hall, honey," Zara said into the phone.

"It's Clary."

"Hey, hun. I'm gonna try the first door in the house to the right. We were just in the left room at the front of the house."

"Okay." I caught Talon's eye and called him over with my hand. He crept over, and as soon as he was close, I told him what Zara said.

On the phone, a door creaked and Zara uttered, "Shoot, it'd be good if the doors were oiled." I held the phone out from my ear so Talon could listen in. "I'm in the room. It's dark and the blinds are drawn. Should I turn on the light?"

"Yeah, Kitten, but make it quick. Take a look around and if he ain't in there, get out."

"Okay."

We heard a click, and then suddenly, Zara gasped, "Blue. Oh my God, Blue. Jason, oh no. No, no." Tears threatened to spill; my hand went over my mouth to control the cry.

"Zara? Kitten, tell us. What do you see?"

"Oh, honey, it's bad. Get in here now. They need help now. Call an ambulance, and get in here *now*."

Talon pulled the phone away and held my hand which gripped the phone. "Listen up. We're going in. There's about five men," he looked to me for confirmation and I nodded, "and they're in the room to the left. We split. You lot take them out; I don't give a fuck how. We're going to the room to the right. It's time to get our brother back. Dodge, call an ambo; we're gonna need it. All right, let's move."

Talon took the phone from my hand and put it to his ear. His eyes closed then bit out, "Fuck," and shut the phone. "Motley's in with Zara. Get the fuck goin'."

Everything went by in a blur then. I ran along with the men to the front of the house. Someone kicked in the front door. Hawks men ran to the left, and Pick, who grabbed my hand, took me to the right. We burst through the door with Talon and Stoke, only to stop dead.

A whimper fell from my mouth.

Blue was slumped over Jason on a mattress on the floor in the corner. He groaned and rolled over, the pain obvious on his bloodied face as he blinked up at us.

Jason lay unconscious on the mattress, and Zara was kneeling next to Blue where Motley stood above them, holding a gun to her head.

"Good to see you all," Blue whispered and gripped his right arm. "But tell me, brother. Why in the fuck are the women here?"

Oh my God, he was hurting, and still, he had time to tell us off.

"Blue," I uttered.

"Sugar." He sighed and closed his eyes.

"Talon," Motley called. "You need to leave and take your men with you."

"I'll be taking Blue and Jason then, as well."

Motley shook his head and smiled. "No, they stay. They're nearly dead anyway, so once you're gone, I'll finish the job."

"No!" I screamed.

"Oh, yes, pretty Clary. Actually, *you* can stay, as well. I like it when things go my way."

I caught Zara's eyes. She nodded to me.

Quickly, she struck out and bit Motley's leg, and that

was when I ran and jumped on him, taking him down to the ground with me. I witnessed Pick covering my man and his brother. Talon was at my side, pulling me off Motley and then shooting him in the stomach. He howled in pain.

Crawling on the dirty carpet, I went to Blue. Taking his hand in mine, I called his name.

Nothing.

No! I rubbed at my eyes to clear them, and with my other hand, I felt for his pulse. It was faint, but there.

"Griz," Talon barked. Griz came flying into the room with Deanna, Killer, and Ivy.

The first thing he said was, "Ambos are close."

"We're gonna have to move them outside. Get the brothers to do some damage to the van. They had an accident. No one is to find these fuckers in here." His vicious glare went from one man to the next. "We take them out ourselves."

"On it," Griz grunted and took off outside.

More commotion started. Throughout it, I stayed with Blue and Jason, even when they moved them outside to lay them on the ground next to the trashed van.

I wasn't really there.

I was numb.

Still, I stayed with Blue, kneeling between the two brothers, a hand in each of theirs. I spoke softly to them, telling them it was all going to be okay.

Jason stirred. He opened his eyes.

"Jason?"

"Clary? Don't tell me you're an angel, too."

I sniffed and snorted. "No, sweetie, no."

"I hurt too much to be dead…." His eyes widened, and he tried to sit up. "Blue, where's Blue?"

Laying my hand on his arm so he'd stay laying on the ground, I said, "He's here. Look, he's right beside you."

"Blue," he uttered. Tears filled his eyes. "He came to save me. He was so brave."

There was no stopping the tears. "I know, Jason, and so were you."

"Blue," he called and reached a hand out to touch his brother's arm. "He saved me, Clary."

"He did, sweetie. He did."

The sirens grew louder and louder, and before the paramedics got to Jason and Blue, Killer knelt down beside Jason and whispered something into his ear.

"Okay, I will."

Two ambulances pulled up to a screeching halt and paramedics raced over; two went to Blue, and two went to Jason. Blue was taken directly onto a stretcher, and before he was wheeled away, I heard a paramedic ask Jason, "What happened here, mate?"

"We had a car accident. I was driving and crashed into that tree there."

ON THE WAY to the hospital, Blue crash-coded. He left me for all of a minute, and it felt like I had lost my own life. I swore my own heart stopped beating. All I wanted to do was hold him, to beg him to stay with me.

I didn't know where anyone else was.

All my thoughts were on Blue.

Willing him to live.

We pulled into emergency at a hospital in Melton, the back doors flew open and Blue was wheeled out. They raced him through other doors and corridors, and all along, I stayed at his side.

"Miss, you have to stay here."

Oh, God.

I couldn't! I didn't want to leave him.

I leaned over to whisper, "You fight, Blue; you need to fight for me, babe. I can't live without you. You're the only one who's shown me how to laugh, live and love. I need you to keep living, to keep showing me, so I can show you what I have in return. You're my perfect, Blue. Please, please... I need you."

"Miss, please, you have to stay."

Someone grabbed my arms, but I tried to fight them off. I needed to stay with my man.

"Darlin', calm, They're taking him to surgery. You can't go in there."

"Griz," I cried.

"Shit, woman, I know."

He knew. They all knew like I did.

Blue looked bad.

He'd left me once.

I had no idea if he would leave me again.

I had never seen so much blood in my life, and that really scared me. It scared me to the point of my heart splitting and threatening to tear apart completely.

"Griz," I sobbed. My hands covered my face until someone spun me around and Griz buried my head against his chest. I gripped tightly to him and broke down like I never had before.

"He's a fighter, darlin'. He'll fight to come back to you."

Oh, God.

My man. My Blue Skies.

EPILOGUE

EIGHT MONTHS LATER

CLARINDA

The day was absolutely beautiful. Deanna stood opposite Griz in a skin-tight, silky white gown. She looked more gorgeous than I had ever seen her, which I suppose wasn't hard since all she usually wore were jeans and tees. Except at work. Every once in a while, she'd switch it up for black pants and a white shirt. Even the large bear of a man Griz looked smashing in a black suit and dark-blue shirt. Of course there was no tie, bikers just didn't do that.

However, my man was more handsome than any other in the church.

His recovery had been hard. The internal injuries took their time to heal, and when that was done, he went through rehab for his broken arm and leg. There were times when he wanted to give up. However, he never did and I was proud of him.

Blue always worried about how his mum was coping after nearly losing her two sons. I'd spoken to her many times and she reassured me she was doing fine because she knew her boys had the Hawks brotherhood at their backs.

She even visited Blue a lot. She knew he needed to see for himself that she wasn't reverting back to what she used to be, and when he saw that, he was content.

Jason was also doing great. It took him a while to get over everything he'd been through, but with the help from all of us, he finally pulled through. He ended up having a late eighteenth birthday party in the bikers' compound in Caroline Springs. His mates thought it was the shit, and the girl he had been trying to impress ended up crashing the party. Jason was stoked. She was sweet and shy, everything I could have hoped for him, and having her at his side made his night that much more special.

Motley and his men were never to be found again. The women and I knew that was going to be the case, especially when Stoke, Killer, Dodge, and Pick stayed back to take care of things at the farmhouse while we got Jason and Blue to the hospital.

I wasn't sure how I felt about knowing they killed them all. If anything, deep down I felt relieved, and if that made me a bad person, then so be it because I was relieved they were no longer a threat to my man or our family.

It was Deanna who said, one girls' night, "You have to learn to live your life the way they live it. If you don't, you'll end up risking what you have with your man. Are you willing to risk that?"

I wasn't and I never would be. Which in turn told me I would learn to be what I had to be and deal with anything that came our way, so I could be with my man always.

"Now," Maya, Zara's beautiful daughter, yelled, bringing me out of my thoughts and back into the church. "Griz, you kiss her now and live happily ever after."

Everyone laughed.

And when Griz brought Deanna into his arms and kissed her passionately, the church erupted in catcalls and hoots. Some even stomped their feet.

The day was wonderful because I got to spend it with my new family.

However, that night was something special.

Blue had brought us home and as soon as we were through the front door, he had my bridesmaid dress over my head and on the floor. I stripped him of his jacket, shirt, and pants.

No words got exchanged between us in that heated moment. Not until Blue had me on the bed with my panties gone and I was sitting on him, riding his dick in my slick pussy. Watching him all day and night had caused me to be soaked.

"Blue...."

"Yeah, sugar?"

"You're marrying me. I thought I should tell you." I moaned and arched as he pushed deep.

He gave me a full belly laugh and said, "Baby, never have I ever known a woman to do the asking, and if my brothers ask, you tell them it was all me. But, fuck yes, I will marry you, even though it wasn't much of a proposal. Though, I suppose you riding my cock is a bonus." He smiled up at me, only it disappeared and he brought me closer down to him.

His hand threaded through my hair, where he gripped hard and rocked us back and forth, so his cock slid in and out of my wet pussy. Then he continued to blow my mind with, "I was gonna ask you, you know... I got the ring and all. I was gonna ask you tomorrow, but you beat me to it. I was gonna ask you because I can't imagine my life without you in it." He kissed me then, our tongues danced together like we had that same night at the wedding, but it was so much more. "Now, you wanna watch me come, or can I do it inside you?" he asked.

I moaned and ground my pussy down deep on his cock, causing him to growl low. "Inside... I'm, oh God. I'm going to come too."

"Good," he clipped, wrapping me tightly to him and thrusting up deep and hard. My pussy walls clamped down around him, and I cried out onto his lips as my orgasm overwhelmed me. "Fuck, baby. Fuck," he mumbled against my lips. His body tensed and then settled as he pumped his seed inside me.

As we relaxed side-by-side, Blue once again continued to blow my mind. "Clarinda," he muttered into the quiet room, besides our ragged breathing.

"Yes, babe?"

"I'm glad I could be the one."

Puzzled, I asked, "The one?"

He rolled to his side and tucked my back into his chest. He kissed my temple then settled down behind me. "The one to chase away your bad dreams, baby. You haven't woken in the middle of the night for a fuckin' long time."

My eyes widened. It was true, and I couldn't believe I hadn't noticed before. It had been months since my nightmares had woken me, screaming in fright.

Months.

I smiled, rolled into him and kissed his chest. "I love you, Blue."

"Love you, too, Sugar. Always."

"Yes, always."

My beautiful, gorgeous biker man was right. He had chased away my tortured past and made my nightmares disappear.

Because he was my new life, he was my saviour in every way, and I couldn't wait to see what our future held.

CHAPTER ONE

STOKE

Another brother laid in the ground. I fuckin' hated this shit. Tank passed a week earlier, and we—his biker brethren—were learning, while sitting in the funeral home, that Tank had a lot of secrets.

And one such secret got him killed.

Another secret shocked the fuck outta all of us.

And that secret sat up at the front of the church, as the funeral director droned on and on about God, Tank and his life.

Tank was one man in the club who I didn't get along with, but still, he was a brother, and I wanted to show my respect for that, which was why I was there.

It was no secret that Tank was shifty, rude, and a bastard to women. But still, he always had our backs, no matter the situation. He loved to party hard, fuck harder and live life on the edge.

Which was how he got himself killed.

Talon knew more about Tank. He was a friend of Tank's, yet, he still didn't know everything there was to know. It was obvious no one in our club did.

Or else someone would have known the fucker was married, and that he was leaving behind two teenage children.

The service finished, and we all moved outside. I stood in a group with Talon, Wildcat, Griz, Deanna, Killer, Chatter, Blue and his woman, of a year, Clary.

"Did anyone know about her?" Blue asked.

A negative note was shared among us.

Looking over Griz's shoulder, my eyes landed on her. Fuck, she was gorgeous. No, I didn't know her at all, but hell, my body wanted to know her in more ways than one.

What a dick move. Thinking of fucking her just as she has put her husband to rest.

Not my fault, she's stunning.

Licking my bottom lip, my eyes travelled over her body where she stood near the doors to the funeral home, as if she was waiting for someone. Her long, light brown hair shone in the late sun's rays. Her curvy body called for my hands. Her green eyes were red-rimmed, but I saw no tears, and since I watched her through the service, I noticed only her children cried quietly at her side. Her body did not indicate that she had cried at all.

Maybe she was fighting it. Maybe she'd break when others weren't around.

Though, for some reason, I had an inkling that wasn't the case.

"Someone needs to bring her into the fold," Wildcat declared.

"Kitten," Talon started.

"No, Honey, look at her. She's standing there protecting her kids, but no one, and I mean no one, has approached her or spoken to her. So, in other words, no one has her back."

Talon rubbed a hand down his face and sighed. "Fuck. Fine. Go do your shit." With that, she beamed, and Wildcat and her posse of pussies started for Tank's misses.

We all watched on, and I was sure we all noticed when Tank's lady saw the women approaching because her whole body stiffened. Her walls were coming up. I couldn't help but wonder why.

Zara held out her hand. Tank's woman looked down at it and said something, bringing her kids closer to her body. Kids who looked to be around about thirteen and sixteen if I had to hazard a guess, the thirteen-year-old a boy and the sixteen-year-old a girl. Both were glaring up at Wildcat and her posse.

She shook her head at whatever Zara said and Deanna stepped forward. I cringed. Hell Mouth was never one to go smooth, or soft, and from the woman's wide eyes, Hell Mouth had just fucked up. Chatter quickly stepped forward and said something, which went on for a while.

Again, she shook her head and said something back. That was when her eyes looked over Zara and landed on our group.

The women turned toward us. Clary was the first to turn back to the woman and say something, causing her to smile slightly, but again, she shook her head.

They were bombing out big time.

It was then the funeral director came out and the widow turned her and her kids away from the pussy posse, and started talking to him.

Wildcat, with a worried look upon her usually smiling face, turned around and started back toward us. In fact, all the women looked as though they were sad or worried.

As soon as they reached us, I asked, "What in the fuck just went down?"

After boss man folded Wildcat into his arms, she said, "She doesn't want anything to do with us."

"How's that, kitten?"

"She's saying she'd just rather be left alone, not that she doesn't appreciate us wanting to lend her a helping hand, but she's fine with her life as is. I get a feeling she doesn't like bikers."

A thought came to me.

"It's time for reinforcements," I said. Talon looked to me, and I added, "Call him. Wildcat, keep an eye on her. If she makes a move to leave, stall...."

"Malinda," Ivy supplied.

With a chin lift, I added, "Stall Malinda until he gets here." It wasn't right the woman was on her own after such a hard situation.

"Right." She nodded. Her and her posse walked closer toward Malinda.

Fucking stunning name. Malinda.

"Jesus, are you sure?" Blue asked.

"He's good at getting in. If anyone can crawl past her walls, it's him."

They all nodded. Talon lifted his phone, pushed a button and put it to his ear. After a second, he spoke into it. "We have a situation. We need you here. Yes, right, okay. Fuck, serious? Yeah. Fine." Talon hung up and groaned. "He'll be here soon."

While we waited, we watched. Thankfully, the funeral director kept Malinda involved in a conversation until we spotted our reinforcement jogging toward us.

"Hey, my lovin' bunch of men. You call and I'm here. What do you need from me besides my body?" Julian asked as he stopped beside Talon.

We all sighed. Julian was the equivalent of an over-excited puppy where you wished he'd just grow the fuck up and stop being annoying. The only problem with that was Julian was never going to grow up.

Still, he was useful, and in tense moments, he knew how to relax them.

I hated to fuckin' say it, and there was no way in hell I would ever tell him, but at times like these, he was good to have around.

Griz filled him in on the situation, and at the end, Julian gripped his chest and a sob tore through him.

"Christ, here we go," Killer mumbled. I chuckled beside him.

"Oh, my God. It warms my gay heart that you all wanted me here to help. Do you think I could patch in the club now, become a member?"

"Julian," Talon growled.

"I was kidding." He smiled and looked over to Malinda. "That beautiful, poor woman. Don't worry about a thing. This gay mama bear will take care of her. Though, we'll need to talk about payment."

"Fuck no! I already agreed you can take the women out on a girls' night, which will no fuckin' doubt end in trouble. Now, you do this or I'll tell Matthew about you offering free butt massages to my brothers."

Julian glared at Talon. "You are a cruel man, Thor. But alas, my boy-toy already knows about that."

"Do you think he wants a reminder?" Talon smirked.

"No," Julian snapped. "You know it took him a month to get over it."

With that, he spun on his heels and trotted over to Malinda and the funeral director. There, he interrupted and introduced himself. The funeral director soon took off, maybe finding Julian a little too much. From then, we watched as Julian flamboyantly worked his magic and had, within seconds, the kids laughing and Malinda smiling.

Now that was a fucking glorious sight to see.

"Women are fucking powerless against him," Griz grumbled.

"Why do they Goddamn love him?" Killer asked.

"Because he brings sunshine into our lives," Clary offered as the women walked up to us. Each man secured their women within their arms.

I did not want any of that shit.

Sex. That was all I cared about.

I'd been stung once, with Helen, Chatter's friend. She was down with gettin' it on with me, but then she realised a biker man wasn't for her. Instead, she went for some uppity college dude, which I didn't know until I found them in bed together. After that, she turned a cold shoulder on me, and since then, hasn't been in Chatter's life as much.

Love and emotional shit were not worth the fucking trouble.

Sticking to just random fuck partners was better.

Then no one got hurt.

Even though I was watching Malinda and I had a need to look out for her, it was all for one reason. I wanted to fuck her.

At least that was what I told myself.

However, from the stormy look, not only from her but from her kids, when they glanced in my direction, it was going to be a hard hunt to partake.

I smiled my megawatt smile and she actually cringed.

Well, fuck!

I then felt like a prick once again because I was trying to con onto her at her fucking husband's funeral.

Yeah, not my best bloody move.

She wasn't going to be worth it, not with kids in tow anyway. I'd never fucked a woman who had kids, so why did I want to start?

I wasn't.

Forget about her and her Goddamn lips that already looked swollen as if she'd been kissed thoroughly.

Forget about her hand on Julian's arm as she smiled shyly up at him. Because I wanted that hand on me and I wanted to rip Julian's arm right off his fucking body for letting her have her hand on him when it should be on me.

Christ. Fuck that shit.

I needed to get out of there and find some dumb bitch to take my hard cock since it had pulsated the moment I laid eyes on Malinda.

Just as I was about to say goodbye, I spotted Julian trotting our way as Malinda led her kids in the other direction.

A smiling Julian stopped beside Griz and announced, "How good am I? Anyone who wants to bow down and kiss my feet may."

Hell Mouth snorted. "No thanks, but you can tell us what went down."

"Malinda and her son, Josh, and her daughter, Nary, are coming to the barbeque tomorrow to celebrate the life of her husband, Tank, at the compound."

"What barbeque?" Wildcat asked.

Julian grinned wide. "The one you now have to organise so we can bring the introvert Malinda and her monsters into our fold. She needs this. Her children need this because I have a feeling they are a handful, and Malinda is at her wit's end. With her hubby now gone, she'll need all the help we can give her."

"You are amazing." Clary giggled.

"Oh, buttercup, thank you. And I think as my reward, I should get a kiss on the cheek from every biker in the club." He tapped his cheek and tilted his head toward Griz.

"No fucking way," Griz growled.

"All right, my women," Zara called. "In light of my hubby losing a brother and in light of taking more into our posse, it's time to get things organised for this get together tomorrow. Who's with me?"

She put her hand in the middle of our circle. Ivy was the first to lay hers on top, then Julian, then Clary and they all turned to look at Hell Mouth.

"Jesus fucking Christ, all right."

She lay her hand on top, and they all took off after layin' some love on their partners.

Once they were out of earshot, Talon turned to us. "Tonight, we meet. We need to figure out all the shit that Tank was involved in. Figure out if his death is cause for us to retaliate, and we need to figure the fuck out if whatever he did, will bring crap to Malinda's doorstep."

With a chin lift, we parted. There was no way I was missing that meet.

CHAPTER TWO

MALINDA

My husband had died. I should be grieving but I wasn't. I should be upset; yet, I wasn't, even though I had just buried him.

Why?

I knew the answer. It was hard to take, to understand,

and some people wouldn't. They'd see me as some cold-hearted bitch. I wasn't. At least I didn't think I was.

Cry dammit.

Nope, nothing.

Feel… but I didn't. I felt nothing.

I pinched myself hard. *There we go.* My eyes started to water.

Only to stop.

Christ.

Terry May, also known as Tank, and I were married when we were both eighteen, when I first become pregnant with our daughter, Nary. In the beginning our marriage was blissful. He treated me as if I was the most precious person in his life. He worked hard, but when he came home, he had time for both Nary and myself. Two years later, Josh came into our lives; again, things were going along great. Yes, we had our little fights, but nothing we both couldn't handle or work through.

It wasn't long after Josh was born when Tank told me he was leaving his old biker club and joining a new one, the Hawks. He thought highly of them, and I wasn't one to argue over a matter like that, not when he was happy to be a part of a club in the first place.

Things changed from there. It was little things to start with. He'd come home drunk, and when Josh would wake from the noise Tank was making, he would become angry, yell and then climb into bed fully-clothed only to pass out. The following day, he wouldn't rise until very late. He be cranky and want to leave the house as soon as he could. I asked him many times what was going on, but he wouldn't tell me. He told me nothing, or that it wasn't any of my business.

A week before my twenty-first birthday, he came home with his brother, Oscar. He walked through the front door and ordered me to take the children out for the day. His brother had always freaked me out; I never liked the way his eyes sought me out. The gleam in them told me he wanted to do bad things, but I was protected, *just*, because I was his brother's wife.

I didn't know what went down that day. They both seemed edgy, yet excited about something. Still, I listened and left with the children.

It was one week later.

One week later, on my twenty-first birthday, I fell out of love with my husband.

Even though he was acting strangely, even though he was moody day after day, I never, not ever, thought my heart could shatter in all but a moment.

And my love for him would die.

But it did.

It did because the night of my twenty-first birthday, I had the children minded by our neighbour, Mrs Cliff. She was a dear old soul and would do anything for a person. So the children went there for the night. I ran around the house in a tizzy, wanting to make everything perfect, because even though it was my birthday, I wanted it special for us. We hadn't bedded one another for at least a month, and I was more than ready.

I dressed in a garter, panties and a sexy hot-pink corset. I remember smiling to myself that night. I was giddy with excitement and thrilled as I thought of what the night would hold.

I was going to get a bit, and my lady bits were crying with glee. "Bow-Chica-Wow-Wow" kept playing over and over in my head.

Until, that was, he came through the front door drunk.

Standing just inside the front door after hearing the loud pipes of his Harley coming down the street, the smile soon flew from my mouth once I saw him staggering.

He took one look at me through hazy eyes and slurred with a vicious voice, "Who in the fuck are you dressed up for?" He took another step in and slammed the door closed. "You expecting your lover to come here?"

"What? No," I cried, annoyed he could even think that. I had only ever been with one man and that man was swaying slightly in front of me.

"Bullshit," he spat. He advanced toward me with hatred in his eyes, and for the first time, I backed away from my husband. "You look like a stupid, fat slut."

"Tank, baby, I did this for you," I said, pain lacing my voice. His words gutted me.

"Well, I don't like my wife looking like the whores I fuck at the club."

A tear ripped through my heart.

"Take it off, *now!*" he bellowed.

I didn't even get a chance to move. He was on me in seconds and tore the clothes roughly from my body. I whimpered and cried as he hands groped hard, pulling all the clothes away.

"Fuck," he hissed. "Even having you naked isn't an improvement. Why in the hell did I marry such an ugly bird?"

My heart cracked open wider from his cruel words.

"Go and put your stupid fucking nightie on. Then I may fuck you. That's if I can even get it up."

"Please don't talk to me like this," I pleaded.

He got close, gripped my jaw in a tight squeeze and barked in my face, "I will talk to you how I want. I will do with you what I like. It's time you learned how to act. You're just the bitch I come home to, who keeps my house clean and takes care of my kids."

"No," I whispered to the ground. I closed my eyes and knew I couldn't take it. I shouldn't take it. With my left hand, I reached up, took hold of his wrist and pushed it from my face. I looked up, glared into his eyes and yelled, "No. You will not do this to me. To us. This isn't you, Tank."

He laughed without humour and slapped me across the face. "Learn your place, bitch. Never talk to me like that again and do as you're fucking told." With that, he shoved me to the ground and repeatedly planted his foot into my stomach, until I was spitting blood from my mouth. He leaned over and hit me twice more in the face. From there, he turned and walked toward the hall where our bedroom lay. Over his shoulder, he said, "Don't bother coming to bed. I don't want you in it. You deserve to sleep on the floor like the dog you are."

I couldn't have moved even if I tried.

That night I lay on the living room floor crying in agonising pain until I passed out.

But before I drifted into unconsciousness, I knew my heart bled more than what flowed from my mouth.

My heart was torn wide open, and from it, my love for the man I married poured out.

It flowed out leaving nothing but agony behind.

That was the day I fell out of love.

Some may think I was crazy to have stayed with him. Some would even understand why I did.

I had my own reasons.

Still, I never really understood them myself.

If I left, I would have lost so much: the house, the money, the safety.

They were ridiculous excuses.

The most ridiculous one was that I didn't want to start over. I didn't want to have to find another man, because what happened if I did and he was worse than Tank?

And really, I was a mother of two children... who would have wanted me?

So I stayed.

I stayed in hope that things would get better. That he would be the husband I knew he could be, had been. That he'd be the father that he could be and had been when Nary was born.

But he didn't. He no longer was.

What also had me staying was because the next morning, when Tank came from the bedroom and spotted me naked, bruised and bloody on the floor, he swore and ran to me.

"Baby, fuck, baby. What happened? Who did this to you?"

He didn't remember.

When I whispered the words, "You." I saw the pain in his eyes. I saw them widen in shock, regret filled him as everything he did came crashing into his mind.

Tears pooled in his eyes. He reached out to my face only to pull back and wince. "Fuck. Christ!" he yelled into the room. He got up from the floor dressed in only boxers and ran down the hall. He came back with a sheet and laid it over my cold body. "Please... fuck, baby. I didn't mean it. I never meant anything I said or did. I couldn't control it. I couldn't stop myself. I was high, baby."

"Hospital," I managed to gasp out.

"Right, of course, fuck."

He got me to the hospital; I had two broken ribs, a fractured cheekbone, and bruises all over. Of course, they questioned how it happened. I used what most women would use in that type of situation—I had fallen down some stairs. Without any witnesses, they couldn't do anything but patch me up and release me.

Tank then went next-door and asked Mrs Cliff to have the children again. He told her I had fallen and hurt myself, and that he needed to take care of me. She did, because there wasn't much Mrs Cliff wouldn't do. She may have been a bit eccentric, but she was sweet and had a safe place for the children to stay.

After that day, Tank was different once again. He wasn't his normal self, like he was when we met. He wasn't that mean, cranky man either. Instead, he was quiet, cold and lifeless. I knew he regretted what he had done to me. Even though he didn't say it, I saw the pain in his eyes. But I couldn't come to forgive him, so I couldn't reassure him.

We lived with each other and that was all.

Even though we slept in the same bed, long gone were the light caresses and touches of love. He slept on his side and me on mine.

We talked calmly to one another, but there were no smiles, no laughter and no love any longer between the two of us.

It had been like that until the day he died.

His body was discovered in bushland. A gunshot wound to the chest, which went straight through his heart. Someone had meant to kill him. I knew this; the police knew this, and I was sure his biker brothers knew this.

What we didn't know was why.

Hope.

That was all I could do, hope that whatever and whoever had caused his death, didn't find its way back to me, to the house and my children.

"Mum?"

Glancing over my shoulder from the front window, to Nary, my sixteen-year-old daughter, I smiled. She looked so much like me. Standing in the kitchen doorway, she had her mobile to her ear.

"Yes, honey?" I smiled.

Should I be smiling? I wasn't sure. I was going crazy with thoughts of how I should act. What would a normal woman do if she lost her husband? I screwed up my face, causing Nary to raise her eyebrows at me. Damn, I just looked weird, so I wiped my face clear and waited to see what she wanted.

"Can I go to Mitch's?"

Closing my eyes, I turned my head back to the window and took a deep breath. I knew the situation would need my full attention so I spun my whole body around. "No, honey. We just buried your dad. I think it's good to stay home, yeah?"

She rolled her eyes. "It's not like it's that big a' deal. He didn't really care about us. Why should we care about him?" said the girl who cried her eyes out in the church.

"Nary, please, just stay home tonight."

"Jesus Christ, Mum."

"Nary!" I yelled. "Watch your mouth." The little shit was getting an attitude, just like I had at her age. I knew how much of a terrible teen I was, so that thought left me cringing.

She glared at me. "Whatever." Then she spun around and said into the phone, "Sorry, Mitch, I have to stay home and pretend I cared about my loser father who treated us all like we were lepers." She snorted. "The warden will let me out tomorrow."

"No," I called. She stomped back into the living room. "We're going to see your father's friends."

"I'm not going," she whined.

She had to. I wanted both Nary and Josh close to me in case anything did arise after their father's death.

"You are, and I don't want to hear more about it. You either do this or no phone for a month," I said.

She gasped. "You wouldn't."

"I would, honey. You know this."

"Why are you being so mean after we buried Dad?"

Oh, God.

Did she not see how funny her saying that was? When only moments ago she said she didn't care.

I knew she did. She knew she did, and we both knew Josh did.

Tonight was for my children. We would reminisce on good times… even if they were few and far between.

ACKNOWLEDGEMENTS

Hot Tree Editing, Becky, Kayla, and Justine. You ladies mean so much to me. Thank you for not thinking my work is too crazy, and also for your support and help through this all xx

Kristin, Jill, Sue, Margreet, Neringa and Amanda for beta reading it for me!

Justine Littleton. You know I love you, woman. I love our messages of just plain crazy shit, and I really can't wait to work alongside you for our next five paranormal novels.

To Mary Manfield, thank you for some awesome, laughable moments in this novel and for all the messages.

To my family, who have supported me through everything.

And a special mention for my monsters. For putting up with a busy mum.

Also Craig thank you for your support, for when I tell you I'm busy and that I have to get this done.

ALSO BY LILA ROSE

Hawks MC: Ballarat Charter

Holding Out (FREE) Zara and Talon

Climbing Out: Griz and Deanna

Finding Out (novella) Killer and Ivy

Black Out: Blue and Clarinda

No Way Out: Stoke and Malinda

Coming Out (novella) Mattie and Julia

Hawks MC: Caroline Springs Charter

The Secret's Out: Pick, Billy and Josie

Hiding Out: Dodge and Willow

Down and Out: Dive and Mena

Living Without: Vicious and Nary

Walkout (novella) Dallas and Melissa

Hear Me Out: Beast and Knife

Breakout (novella) Handle and Della

Fallout: Fang and Poppy

Standalones related to the Hawks MC

Out of the Blue (Lan, Easton, and Parker's story)

Out Gamed (novella) (Nancy and Gamer's story)

Outplayed (novella) (Violet and Travis's story)

Romantic comedies

Making Changes

Making Sense

Fumbled Love

Trinity Love Series

Left to Chance

Love of Liberty (novella)

Paranormal

Death (with Justine Littleton)

In The Dark

CONNECT WITH THE AUTHOR

Webpage: www.lilarosebooks.com

Facebook: http://bit.ly/2du0taO

Instagram: www.instagram.com/lilarose78/

Goodreads:
www.goodreads.com/author/show/7236200.Lila_Rose

CPSIA information can be obtained
at www.ICGtesting.com
Printed in the USA
BVHW062255081122
651520BV00008B/47